HOW THEY FELL

A FALLING WARRIORS SERIES NOVELLA

FALLING WARRIORS
They don't love—they own.

NICOLE RENÉ

CREATING ALPHA MALES YOU HATE TO LOVE.

VISIT MY WEBSITE AT——www.authornicolerene.com

Cover Design & Interior Formatting— © T.E Black Designs;
www.teblackdesigns.com

Photography by © Joel Hicks Creative Enterprises;
www.joelhicksbookcovers.com

Models: © Joel Hicks and Tillie Feather

DEDICATION

To my readers who first fell in love with Xavier and Leawyn. Words cannot express my gratitude to you. Thank you.

GLOSSARY

Leawyn: Lee-uh-wen
Namoriee: Nem-or-ree
Tyronian: Ty-row-nian
Xillik: Xi-lick
Ryder: Rider
Rhoxon: Row-han
Lévaunia: Lay-von-nia
Tyberious: Ty-beer-ious
Trixus: Trix-us
Titus: Ty-duss
Viktorious: Victorious
Cixrus: Cy-russ
Torrick: Tor-rick
Alissowyn: Alis-oh-wen
Izayges: Iz-uh-ges
Siraces: Sir-aces
Asori: Uh-sor-ree

INDEX

PROVA SINAVI: The trial for warriors in training where they have to hunt and capture a tribe prisoner and bring them back to the tribe and execute them. Those who fail are shamed and will never be a warrior, the greatest honor for Samaritan tribes.

CHAPTER ONE

S HE WAS RUNNING. HEART POUNDING, her lungs heaved with strain, but she didn't stop.

She couldn't.

Her eyes stayed glued to the two fighting forms up ahead on the hill.

She needed to get to them.

Almost there...

They dove toward the ground. One reached the sword first; turned toward the other.

Raised it.

"No!"

But it was too late.

CHAPTER TWO

WANDERING HANDS WOKE HER UP. Someone had pulled the covers off her and now calloused fingers were gripping her knees, rolling her onto her back. Hair tickled her inner thighs, and she felt warm breath on her folds until…

"Xavier," Leawyn sighed, her back arching when he gave her slit another long lick, warming her up with the slow stirs of pleasure.

"Hmmm." The vibration of his hum sent an electric shock through her sensitive flesh which made her shiver. She buried her hands in his hair, clutching his scalp to her now gyrating hips, trying to force him to use more pressure.

He was in one of his teasing moods; he wasn't going to make it easy for her.

The bastard.

"Tell me what you want, Leawyn," he rumbled, dodging her attempts to bring his mouth back onto her slick flesh. He brought his hand up, sinking a finger inside of her, teasing her by pumping the digit with slow, deliberate movements.

"You know what I want." She moaned when his thumb tapped her *there*

"Give me the words," he ordered. "Give them to me, and I'll let you come."

That was Xavier to the core. He'll *let* her come—not *make* her come.

Demanding.

Dominating.

Hers.

She knew what he wanted to hear—he made her say it often—and there were some days that he needed to hear it more than others. Ever since the war, there was another dynamic in their relationship. He was still Xavier, but she knew she was privy to a side of him that he allowed only her to see.

But right now, she didn't want that side. She wanted to come.

So, she gave him what he wanted. She submitted.

"I love you," she groaned, the need unbearable now. "I belong to you."

"Good girl." Then his mouth lowered completely on her, and she was lost.

"How did everything go?" Leawyn asked, turning to find Xavier still gloriously naked. Shamelessly, she ogled her husband. After Xavier had *let* her come from his mouth, he wasted no time in crawling over her body and taking her.

Their lovemaking was passionate, and hot, but it lacked the roughness she desired and what he usually provided in their joining.

Any gentleness Xavier was able to possess, she had taught him. Her husband was fierce and brutal, being the most feared man of all the tribes. He was a natural born killer, a strict leader, and a formidable opponent. When Leawyn was told that she was to marry him at just eighteen years old, she thought her life was over.

To say their marriage was tremulous in the beginning, would have been a vast understatement.

It was filled with hate, jealousy, resentment, fear and—eventually—love.

However, unconventional it may have been.

Xavier stopped, and she caught the stiffness of his shoulders before he relaxed. His expression was impassive when he turned to regard her. Her eyes dropped down—she couldn't help it! —then flashed back to his face, which smirked at her.

"See something you like?"

"Perhaps," she replied coyly. She watched his nostrils flare, the familiar glint entering his eyes whenever she challenged him. Xavier's favorite thing to do was remind her who exactly she belonged to. She's not ashamed to admit that sometimes she provoked him purposely, wanting his dominance.

And the orgasms that usually followed.

He stepped toward her and her pulse spiked, body tensing in anticipation. His gaze landed on her stomach and the bulge she'll soon no longer be able to cover with strategically picked dresses.

Her shoulders sagged in disappointment when his demeanor changed, and instead of throwing her back on the bed and ravishing her like she wanted him to, he opted to turn around and finish getting dressed.

She watched him come over to her once he finished, tilting her chin with his thumb before pressing his lips to hers.

"It went well," he answered her original question. "You taste good," he murmured against her lips, giving her another kiss.

"I taste like you."

He hummed before stealing three more kisses. "Take it easy today," he ordered, pulling away. "I better see you napping come mid-day."

"And if I don't?"

"Then I'll come collect you myself and—"

"Spank me?" she supplied hopefully. Xavier chuckled.

"Just behave, wife," he growled playfully. He gave her one last quick peck then walked out the door.

She sighed, feeling dejected. She shouldn't feel the way she did. After all, they had made love just earlier, but ever since she had started to show in her pregnancy, something within Xavier changed.

There was a time when she had wished for Xavier to be gentle with her...it seemed the fates finally decided to grant her wish.

So why did that bother her so much?

XAVIER DIDN'T SPANK HER WHEN HE CAUGHT HER NOT-NAPPING during the mid-day. He did, however, throw her over his shoulder and march her back into their home and proceeded to undress her, make love to her, then take a nap with her. It was a happy surprise. They didn't get to spend their days together too often, so when they did, she treasured those precious moments.

Even if it was while sleeping in her husband's arms.

When she woke, Xavier was gone and, in his place, Namoriee was lounging around her hut quietly cleaning.

"How late is it?" Leawyn asked mid-yawn. Namoriee startled and dropped whatever was in her hand. The contents shattered; Namoriee cursed.

"Sorry," she winced.

"It's a-alright, milady," Namoriee said, crouching down to the mess. While Namoriee cleaned, Leawyn used that time to pull on the robe that was waiting for her at the end of the bed.

Namoriee stood and barely managed to stop herself from colliding into Leawyn, who had come to help her. Leawyn couldn't help but giggle at the exasperated look that Namoriee shot her.

Namoriee had this uncanny skill of portraying everything that she was feeling with just one look. Sixteen, extremely shy, and with a stutter, she had hardly spoke when she first became her hand-maiden. Nowadays, she was speaking more despite her disability, and Leawyn couldn't have been prouder.

The tribe deserved to know how sweet and witty her friend was.

"Hope this isn't t-t-too important?" Namoriee asked, motioning to the pieces she held in her hand.

"A bowl?" Leawyn's brow arched. "I think we'll live," she finished dryly.

They hung out in her hut for a while before they decided to go out and walk around the village to see where Leawyn was needed. Being the lady chief of the tribe, she made it a point to be more active in the day to day activities of her people. She often played mediator for disputes between the tribes' members and helped clean up the village and restore it to its once former glory.

"I think this place is ready to go!" Leawyn beamed, looking around at the giant structure she was in that would serve as the Izayges dining hall. Castic, who had just come from his training to help, looked over at Leawyn.

"This was a grand idea, Lady Chief. I'm glad this was built." He smiled, and Leawyn was momentarily blinded at how much more handsome it made him look. Everyday, he started to look older to her. More grown up. It made her both proud, and sad. Though Castic was not her son, she's always had a soft spot for the boy. Overcome with emotion, she hugged him.

"Oh Castic, you're becoming so handsome!"

"Ugh, Lady Chief—you're embarrassing me!" Castic complained, trying to dodge the kisses she was now smothering his cheek with.

With a wide grin, Leawyn stopped her torture and watched in amusement when he instantly swiped at his cheek. His face still flushed, he superstitiously looked around to make sure none of his friends saw.

"Shall we announce a feast tonight?" Namoriee asked, smiling.

Leawyn looked everything over with a clinical eye, making sure that they were, in fact, ready. Finding that only minor touches were needed, she turned to Namoriee.

"If our hunters can hunt more meat, I don't see why not!"

The people around her cheered, and she couldn't help but laugh at their excitement.

"I'll go tell Xavier," she said, turning to do just that when a gentle hand stopped her.

"Why don't I t-t-tell him?"

"Are you feeling well?' she asked, surprised at Namoriee's offer. Namoriee was terrified of her husband.

"Y-yes. I just think you would be more useful h-here. Y'know, p-p-planning."

Leawyn wasn't convinced. She studied Namoriee, trying to read her secrets on her face but Namoriee kept her look innocent enough to ensure Leawyn that she wasn't innocent at all. She was still suspicious, but she shrugged.

"Go ahead."

With a quick thanks and timid smile, Leawyn watched her go.

"THE CHIEFS OF THE OTHER tribes can finally confirm their losses," Tyronian said, coming to stand in front of the table. "Four hundred dead. Hundred from the Siraces, two-hundred from the Asori, and a hundred of our own men," Tyronian reported solemnly.

Xavier rubbed his temples, trying to stop the headache from forming. His shoulders were heavy, weighted with the knowledge of the deaths of good warriors. It's been close to five months since the war of the tribes, and they were still feeling the aftereffects. When Xavier and the Izayges warriors came home from the battlefield, it was to find that the Izayges village had been attacked. While the damage wasn't annihilation, it was extensive. Huts had to be rebuilt, and non-warrior members lives had been lost.

"What else?"

"Restructure of the village is almost complete. Most of the huts lost have been restored, our hunters have gathered more of the animals we'd lost, and the dinning hut you requested is half-way done."

"Good," Xavier paused. "And the survivors?"

Tyronian's expression leveled. "They're prisoners now."

"Make sure they stay alive, but not live comfortably. Divide them and transport them to the Siraces and Asori to do what they will. We'll use them for *Prova Sinavi.*"

"As you command," Tyronian nodded, pivoting to do what he asked. He hesitated then turned back to him. "How's Leawyn?"

Xavier's expression darkened, a frown forming. It was obvious that he was troubled.

"She continues to have nightmares, but she either has no memory of them, or chooses to pretend she doesn't scream every night."

Like a coward, he avoided looking at Tyronian, unwilling to see his sympathy. It was hard enough for Xavier to admit that he felt helpless—something he did not allow himself to feel.

But he *did* feel helpless, because his wife was hurting and there was nothing he could do.

And he hated it.

"Have you tried…talking to her?"

At his flat look, Tyronian chuckled, holding his hands up in surrender. "Of course, how silly of me. You're Xavier—big and mean and by no means a communicator."

Xavier prided himself for not rolling his eyes. Even if Tyronian had a point.

"Are you done?" Xavier grumped.

"Never."

Tyronian only grinned at his growl of annoyance, but then became serious.

"Don't wait too long. You're not the only one who's seen through her facade. She's lost weight, something she can't afford to lose right now. If not for her, then think about your child."

Tyronian and Namoriee were the only ones who knew about her pregnancy. Since his younger brother Tristan took off, he hasn't been able to tell him that he would be an uncle. Thinking about Tristan still caused a pain in his chest. Things had changed between them after he got married, a rift that just seemed to grow with each passing day.

He couldn't help but feel guilty that perhaps he was the reason Tristan ran away on his quest of "self-discovery" as Leawyn put it. Whatever that meant.

He wouldn't admit it aloud, but he missed his brother. He wanted him to come home where he belonged.

"I'll handle my wife how I see fit," Xavier said finally.

"I have no doubt about that," Tyronian grinned. He didn't say anything further, and Xavier watched him walk out the door. He didn't know how long he sat there staring at the wall, his thoughts consumed with his wife and brother when the door opened, and in walked the last person he expected.

"Namoriee," he greeted, his tone belied his surprise.

He watched her shut the door, and shuffled closer to him, her expression displaying her nerves clearly. His glance down at her hands—that were fiddling, and anxious—was indiscernible, and by the time she was upon him, he gathered everything he needed to know, just from her body language.

She was here with a purpose, one that she believed in enough to face him—because he knew that she was terrified of him, something he was content to not rectify—but she was nervous. Afraid.

He watched her as she seemed to battle with herself, before she pushed her shoulders back and stood straighter.

"The d-dining h-h-h-hut is complete," she told him. "Leawyn w-w-wishes to have a f-feast tonight."

"Okay." He eyed her, noting that her gaze was no longer alternating between his eyes and her feet.

She didn't elaborate, nor did she continue to carry conversation. If she had come all this way to only tell him about the feast, you'd think she would leave after delivering the message. But she didn't. Instead, he was left staring at a girl who annoyed him on most days, but tolerated on others because she was his wife's best friend. But he wasn't a patient man, and he didn't like useless silences.

His temper was notorious, and quick—something Namoriee was about to experience until she spoke.

"I'm worried about Leawyn."

"Why?

She looked up at him then, and something shifted inside his chest at the emotion on her face. "She smiles, and laughs, but it's fake, or...not full." She made a frustrated sound, as if annoyed with herself. But what he found interesting was that her speech didn't halt like it usually did. He wondered if she even realized that it always seemed to disappear when she was passionate about something.

"She's different. She's been different ever since..." she stopped, her face paling in fear. But she didn't have to finish because he knew what she was going to say. He felt the familiar fury fill him when he thought of before. Of the night that Leawyn saved his life.

The monster inside of him relished in Namoriee's fear, which he could plainly see when he took a threatening step toward her. He had never understood his wife's friendship with this girl; Leawyn was so much stronger than her. Namoriee was weak, and easily scared. She kept her head down, content to float through life as invisible as possible. But then he started to understand why Leawyn kept her in her company throughout their marriage.

Namoriee was loyal, and showed silent strength that differed from Leawyn's. Namoriee was a dog in a den of wolves. She showed teeth and could bite just as hard when put into a corner.

Her swallow was audible, and though she trembled ever so slightly, her wide-eyed gaze didn't shy from his, nor did she step back even when he crowded into her space.

He had to respect that.

"You were going to say *his* name, weren't you?"

Mutely, she nodded.

"You are aware that I forbade his name to ever be spoken, are you not?" He snarled.

"Then I s-s-suppose that it is a g-g-good thing I didn't say it a-aloud, then."

He covered his shock at her cheek by keeping his glare steady. Her eyes widened as if she herself couldn't believe she snarked him. He stared her down a moment longer, then showed her his back when he turned away, effectively dismissing her.

"You may leave now."

She hesitated, then "What about Leawyn?"

He glanced over at her. "I will handle my wife." It was an ominous promise, and she knew it.

Her expression shuttered, and she didn't argue, because she knew she couldn't. Instead, she gave him a respectful nod and hurried out of his sight.

He plopped back down on his chair, running a hand through his hair in his frustration. A part of him had held hope that he was simply overeating, that his guilt had somehow made him see Leawyn differently. But Namoriee coming to him just confirmed that he wasn't wrong.

She changed.

Her light was dimming. Like a flicker of a candle struggling to withstand the wind.

He was losing her.

He swore to fight for her.

But…how could he fight a ghost?

CHAPTER THREE

EAWYN DIDN'T KNOW WHAT THE Izayges were like before her and Xavier got married, but when she looked across all the smiling and happy faces as they ate and danced inside of the newly built dining hut, she couldn't imagine a time with anything less that what she saw right at this moment.

"He's a p-pig."

She turned to Namoriee who had spoken, following her line of sight. She understood what caused her scorn immediately.

"He's Tyronian. Pig wouldn't exactly be my first choice."

Namoriee leveled her a look. "Who's s-s-side are you on anyways?"

She held back her smile. "If I didn't know any better, I would think you're jealous, Namoriee."

Namoriee's expression pinched, as if the very notion made her feel sick. But Leawyn wasn't fooled. She looked back to Tyronian, who valiantly tried to hide the fact his eyes weren't already glued to them by turning his attention to the sandy-brunette sitting on his lap.

She glanced at Namoriee discretely and, just as she thought she thought, she was watching Tyronian, too.

"You could go over to him," Leawyn said, catching Namoriee's attention. "I'm sure he would much rather have you on his lap."

"I've already sat on his lap," she deadpanned. "It was m-mortifying."

She didn't say anything more, and once she helped settle her into her chair, she left; walking in a different direction than they came in.

Leawyn couldn't say she was surprised when the girl on Tyronian's lap was called away by Tanna and redirected to a different man.

Not jealous, Namoriee had said.

Leawyn laughed.

FOR THE WHAT SEEMED TO be the umpteenth time, Leawyn surveyed the room. Almost everyone was done with their meal; content to bask in the company of their tribesmen and the willing women who warmed the men's laps. She glanced at the plate on her right that was still filled with food that she had saved for her husband.

Where is he? She thought, gnawing on her bottom lip in worry.

More time passed, and just when she was about to pack up his meal to search for him, he walked in. She watched him scan the place, knowing that he was taking everything in with a vivid eye that was second nature to him. She had no doubt that he was making note of every person, every exit, every potential threat. Even if they were in times of what seemed like peace, Xavier was always on the alert. Peace didn't exist for him, and she knew, deep in her bones, that the only time he would ever find *true* peace was in his death.

His eyes landed on her, and she didn't try and hide the shudder that went through her. Xavier's eyes could be the thing of nightmares, or the thing of dreams. In the beginning, his eyes scared her. How he looked at people.. it was like staring into vacant depths. No fear. No victory. No emotion.

Warrior eyes.

But then, there was something else. Something...*primal.* With just one look, he could make her pulse spike. The darkness that always brewed inside the irises, turned into a fire that she swore she could feel directly inside of womb when directed at her.

His stare didn't waver even as he started his prowl toward her. A slow crawl of pleasure slithered through her body, starting from her toes and moving up. By the time he was in front of her, she was practically panting.

"Leawyn," he said, his voice a natural gruttal timber. She had to tilt her head back to look him in the eye. His perusal of her was naturally seductive with its familiarity. He knew every inch of her body. Knew every spot to touch to inflict both pain, and pleasure.

She licked her lips, her mouth suddenly gone dry with her arousal. He watched her tongue glide against the plumpness, and she revelled in how his pupils dilated. His eyes lifted and met her own.

It was ludicrous, really. How he easily he could turn her on with just one look.

"Xavier."

He smirked, knowing that the tremor in her response wasn't because of fear. He slid an escaped tendril of her hair behind her ear. Her hair was so long now, it cascaded past her buttucks. Too long a length for the heat of the day, so she had tied it up with leather so that it was off her neck.

He nudged his chin at the plate of food. "You eat?"

"I was saving that for you."

He nodded once, then reached for her hand. It was enormous compared to her own. She stood, rounding the table to him. His long legs ate up the distance, drawing them away from the dining hut, and the main tier of the village. She didn't question him, simply content to follow him.

"Xavier," she said quietly. He was walking too fast, and it was hard for her to keep up. Mid-stride he turned, reaching for her. She giggled when he swept her up, cradling her against his chest. She drew his mouth to hers, groaning quietly when his tongue ruined the chances of her kiss being sweet by entwining with her own. They continued to kiss as he carried her until she was certain that she was going to die just from the need.

Rushing water met her ears, and she smiled against his mouth, their destination apparent. She pulled away from their kiss to look at the waterfall that the village used to bathe.

She turned to him. "You trying to tell me I stink?"

He chuckled quietly, setting her down on her feet. He stepped back, and she felt his stare like it was a caress.

"Strip."

The command brought forth a memory. He had ordered her to do the same once, in this exact location. She shivered, but instead of feeling the need to meet the challenge in his eyes like last time, all she felt was giddiness. She quickly complied, enjoying how each article of clothing she removed affected him. When she stood shamelessly naked in front of him, she looked to him for direction. He tilted his head down at himself, his voice husky when he ordered, "take my clothes off."

Greedily, she complied. Xavier very rarely wore a shirt, so it took her no time at all to relieve him of his belt and pants, bearing his erection. She cupped it, running her hands down the base and up so that her thumb could brush against the head. He hissed out a breath, his eyes closing in enjoyment. She played with him for awhile until he gripped her wrist, stilling her.

He hauled her up his body only with one arm, making her equally amazed and aroused at his brute strength. Her legs wrapped around his trim waist, her lips molding to his while he walked them into the water. When he was in waist deep, he pulled away from their kiss to stare into her eyes.

"Don't abuse your head-start."

She frowned. "What?"

At his smirk, her eyes widened. "Xavier don't you dar—" she cut off with a scream when he launched her in the air, tossing her into the lake. She came up with a gasp, throwing water at his laughing form.

"You bastard!" She screamed at him, laughing.

"Better start swimming," he called out to her. She shrieked when he dived into the water and started to swim to the waterfall as fast as she could. She climbed up the first rock, scrambling her way up. She squealed when he snatched her up mid-climb, throwing her over his shoulder as he climbed the rest of the way, carrying her. She was still giggling when he set her down on her feet, encompassing her waist with his hands. He pulled her close, his laughing eyes staring down into her own.

"Do you remember the first time we came here together?"

They were standing on a large, flat rock that was slick with water and splattered with moss. A smaller waterfall was behind them, the leftover trickle of the massive one in front of them that cascaded down into the lake below.

"Yes," she replied, her hand gilded and dipped over the contours of the muscles in his arm. Her smile was soft with the memory and pain. "It was the night you were attacked."

His head tilted at her answer, a question in his eyes. He wanted to know why she left out the real reason she had dragged him here that night. He gripped her waist tighter, not quite painful, but enough to let her know that he was displeased with her without having to utter the words.

It was silent between them, the only noise coming from the waterfall in front of them. She could feel him watching her, but like a coward, she couldn't bring herself to meet his gaze. She was frustrated with herself.

A plethora of emotions battled with her heart and mind everyday. She wanted her husband so much. Craved his attention, his touch—both inflicting and tender—wanted to just *be* with him without the tension of impending battle and doom. It's been months since the war, yet...

Don't make me do this.

You won't shoot me, Lea.

She closed her eyes, fighting a shudder.

"I think it was here that I started to realize I was falling in love with you. Though at the time, I didn't know the meaning of the word."

Her eyes flew open in surprise.

"Here?"

He nodded. "I threatened you. I was covered in blood, but you had looked at me like no else had. You didn't fear me...you didn't recoil in disgust. You simply accepted me, even knowing that there was blood of someone's life staining my hands. Accepted me knowing that I was a killer. That night changed everything for me, Leawyn."

He lifted her chin with his thumb and cupped the side of her face.

"You saw the monster, and you saw the man. That night I saw you more than just my wife...I saw you as an ally."

She didn't realize a tear had slipped her eye until he caught it with his thumb, banishing its existence with a swipe of her cheek. He stepped closer to her, his hand still cupping her cheeks. He started at her heavily, a hidden message there filled with silent declarations and pleas.

"Tell me what's wrong."

"There's nothing wrong." It was a blatant lie.

"I don't believe you," he whispered, nuzzling her brow. She reached up, standing on her tiptoes and clutched his neck. She slid her hands into his hair that was wild, and unkempt—just like him.

"You don't have to believe me," she whispered back. "You just have to trust me."

She shuddered in desire when he spun her around. Her hands slapped on the wet rocks the same time he tugged her back by her hair, arching her neck.

"You want me to trust you?" He growled. "Yet you don't do the same. There are no secrets between us, Leawyn. Your secrets are mine. Your truths are mine. Your dreams, and your nightmares. Everything. Is. Mine."

He accentuated his words with a thrust of his hips, impaling himself deep inside her. Her spine zinged with pleasure, and she groaned at the stretch. Water cascaded over her, between her breasts, over her peaked nipples, and down her navel. Xavier gripped her neck with just enough pressure to remind her how destructive his hands could be if he wanted. His thumb pushed past her lips on her moan, thrusting inside her throat in tandem with his hips, making her gag the slightest bit. His other hand snaked around her waist and traveled down, past the corse, blonde curls and into the treasure only he had the map to. She whimpered when he parted her folds, his thumb pressing against her slick, swollen nub.

One touch; teasing.

Two; assertive.

Three; demanding.

Then, he pinched her, shocking her. Hurting her. *Pleasing* her.

It was too much.

She came on a gargled scream around his limb still inside her throat. Xavier thrust inside of her harder, his skin slapping against her own. The thrusts weren't brutal—he's taken her far worse. Deeper and more painful—but they were relentless, making her gasp for breath. Her legs were shaking, struggling not to buckle. His hand left her mound to grab her inner-thigh tight enough to leave bruises, lifting her leg high, and out so that she was balancing on one leg.

It made him go deeper, stroking the spot inside her that made her wonton.

"Xavier!"

"You got something to say to me?"

She shook her head, expression pinched. She couldn't tell him, because she was afraid to admit her weakness.

"Then silence. Not another word from you, Leawyn."

She moaned, nails scraping against the stone. It felt like days as he pounded into her from behind, his hands alternating between gripping her nape, and her waist. Twice now, he had flicked her clitoris, strumming and priming her for an orgasm, only to pull away each time she was about to climax. When he did it a third time, she screamed out her frustration. He was punishing her.

"Please," she whimpered.

Xavier grew still, and with horror she realized what she did.

She spoke.

"Naughty girl," he hissed in her ear. Then she was spun around, forced to her knees. Her mouth spread wide around his thick length when he pushed into her mouth fluidly, the tip going deep and activating her gag reflex. It seemed so brutal, but his movements were slow. He took her mouth like it was his salvation, and her penance.

"Swallow every drop," he panted, thrusted harder, desperately.

Her eyes stung—both from tears, and the water that trickled from her temple—and her head hit the rock every so often with each movement of his hips. Xavier reached down, grabbed either side of her head, and yanked her to him so that her chin was flush against his sac. His cock jerked, then come jetted down her throat. She choked, trying to swallow around him. Xavier groaned, keeping her captive until every last drop was expelled. Only then did he pull away, and his hands became gentle. He looked down at her, lids heavy and sated.

"Open your mouth, pretty girl."

She did, knowing what he was checking. When he was satisfied, he bent, picking her up.

"You don't get to come tonight. Do you know why?"

She nodded her head, but at his disapproving look, she stopped. "Because I spoke."

He shook his head, and her confusion must have shown. "You don't get to come because you chose to hide from me, instead of confide in me. And Leawyn?" She lifted her gaze from over his shoulder. Their eyes met.

"I know something is wrong, but I won't push you. But know this." He picked her up by her arms, bringing them nose to nose. He smoothed back her wet hair, gripping the tresses. His eyes were bottomless pools of dark soil compared to her ocean blues.

"You can't hide from me forever. My monster is bigger and meaner than yours and it will drag yours out kicking and screaming if it has to. That's not a threat—it's a promise."

She knew it, too. Her time was limited.

CHAPTER FOUR

WEEKS HAD PASSED SINCE THEIR time at the lake, and Leawyn and Xavier found themselves spending more time apart by chance. Tyronian had been sent on a mission to the Siraces tribe, while Xavier was away on some mysterious business he didn't feel the need to disclose to Leawyn.

Something they had fought about, which had left her in a miserable mood for days. Namoriee—bless her—noticed this and had suggested that they go on a ride together.

Desperate to go out, she had agreed. Leawyn had missed being able to just ride for pleasure, the last few months had been so desperate, so quick. They rode for a purpose, for survival. She missed the days where she felt free, with the wind in her hair and the trust of her mare as they explored life together.

Namoriee was on a buckskin mare, who easily kept pace with them as they charged forward. Leawyn looked over at her, shooting her a matching smile before she steered Deydrey to the left, Namoriee and her horse following. Gradually, they slowed their pace until they both were walking leisurely side by side. They stopped atop the cliff in the woods that had a birds-eye view of their village.

They sat in companionable silence for a bit, until Leawyn sighed.

"Out with it, Namoriee."

She caught Namoriee looking at her from the corner of her eye for awhile now, as if she wanted to say something, but didn't.

Namoriee blushed, looking sheepish. "Sorry."

"Well?" she looked at her expectantly. "What's on your mind?"

Her friend hesitated, worrying her bottom lip. She waited, knowing that her friend took a while to gather her thoughts and gain confidence to speak her mind. It might not seem like it, but Namoriee had changed and matured so much in the small amount of time Leawyn had known her.

When she first met her, she was skittish, and struggled with her speech and was afraid of her own shadow. But underneath, she had a heart worth thousands of the best stallions, and fiercely loyal. Leawyn knew that her life would have been much worse in the Izayges if it wasn't for her.

"Are you h-h-happy, lady chief?"

Leawyn was surprised by that question. "Yes, Namoriee. Why do you ask?"

"You seem different."

"How?" she asked, trying to curve her defensiveness.

"You smile but it d-d-doesn't reach your eyes. You l-l-laugh, but it doesn't sound joyful. It sounds s-s-strained. You just..." Namoriee trailed off, looking down at her hands.

The horses they were on were grazing, and Leawyn had to gently urge Deydrey back when she started to stray for a fresher patch of grass.

"Are you happy?"

Leawyn contemplated that question. *Was* she happy? At times, she could believe she was. But there were times when the past haunted her. When the memories that were stomped down by adrenaline and survival started to surface, crawling to the forefront of her mind like a corpse rising from the dead, forcefully fighting to escape it's grave.

Memories that she fought against and hid from.

It was a battle that she fought daily, and she was losing.

But she couldn't admit that. To anyone...even herself.

"I'm happy," she lied. "You shouldn't worry. I just haven't been feeling good."

Namoriee seemed relieved with her answer, and it made her guilt taste like the worst poison.

"That's normal," Namoriee smiled. "The baby will no doubt control everything about you in the coming days. I'm so excited for you. The Goddess has blessed us indeed in our time of needing some joy."

"Yes," Leawyn smiled, though it was forced. She looked away from her friend's trusting eyes and toward the horizon that was glowing with the promise of sunset.

"Yes, she did."

WHEN THEY GOT BACK AND had taken care of their horses it was around supper, so they started to trek the path to the dining hut. They were halfway there when they spotted two forms, one of which was huddled and hugging their knees. They looked at each other and slowed, realizing that it was Castic and Garnette.

"Garnette? What's the matter?" Leawyn asked in concern once they were within range. Castic looked up at her, an angry scowl on his face and a storm in his eyes that was surprising.

"I found her like this. She won't tell me what's wrong."

Leawyn looked at her, frowning in concern at the sight of her tears. Garnette was young, but she was always amazed at how strong she was. She very rarely cried. Something terrible must have happened. She crouched next to Castic, who stood to make room for her. His arms folded across his chest, and he looked at his friend with both distress and anger—though she knew it wasn't directed at Garnette.

Leawyn smiled softly at Garnette, smoothing her hair away so that she could better see her face.

"Tell me what's wrong, Gar."

Garnette sniffled, lifting her head from her knees just a bit. "Nothing."

It was barely noticeable, but Leawyn saw her eyes shoot to Castic before looking back down.

"Castic," Leawyn said, tilting her head to look at him. "Do you think you could give us a moment? Maybe go fetch Garnette a wet rag so that she may wash her face?"

Castic's frown deepened. It was clear that he didn't want to leave.

"Please?"

He hesitated, but at Leawyn's look, his shoulders slumped.

"Yeah, sure," he grumbled dejectedly. He glanced at Garnette one more time before he went and did as she asked at a run. Leawyn turned back to Garnette.

"Now will you tell me what has you so upset?"

"It's stupid," Garnette sniffed, wiping her tears and nose with the back of her hand.

Leawyn squeezed her kneecaps. "I don't think anything that is able to make you cry will be stupid, Garnette."

Garnette's lip wobbled. "I saw Castic kissing a girl."

She heard Namoriee suck in a breath, but she ignored her. She tilted Garnette's chin up so that she met her eyes. Her heart squeezing at the sight of her red-rimmed eyes.

"When?" she asked softly.

"Tonight. I was looking for him. Ever since the Warrior Choosing we haven't got to play as much. But he promised me we would today." Garnette's eyes filled with tears anew. "But when he didn't show, I lookded for him. That's when I..." she cut off, crying.

"Oh, sweet girl," Leawyn sighed, moving so that she was sitting on the floor with Garnette and held her close.

"He lefted me, Lady Chief. He doesn't want to hang out with me anymore!"

"Don't be silly," Leawyn chastised. "Castic loves you. He'd never *not* want to hang out with you."

"Then why did he kiss her instead of playing with me?" Garnette hiccupped around her crying.

"Garnette, what you're feeling is jealousy," Leawyn explained patiently.

"J-jealousy?"

"Yes," Leawyn replied, wiping one of her tears away. "When you saw Castic kissing that girl, how did it make you feel?"

"Angry and sad. I didn't like it."

Leawyn tried not to smile, but it was nearly impossible. Garnette was just so cute. As was Castic's friendship with her. She had seen firsthand how much Castic adored and protected Garnette, who didn't understand that most boys his age wouldn't want to hang out with someone her age. But Castic did so willingly.

It was adorable.

She was afraid that something like this would happen. Leawyn knew it was only a matter of time that Castic would start to take an interest in girls, and Garnette was bound to get her feelings hurt.

"That's jealousy," Leawyn explained gently. "You're used to having Castic to yourself, and now that that is changing, it's upsetting you. But Garnette, as painful as it may be, you're going to have to get used to this. Castic is becoming a man and wanting to...kiss"—she winced—"girls is part of him doing so. You need to understand that."

"I don't *like* it! I don't want him to do that! Why did he have to be a stupid warrior anyways? Why couldn't he just be my friend?"

"Shh," Leawyn soothed when Garnette started to get really

worked up. She waited for her to stop crying before she continued. "Garnette, you need to be happy for Castic. You're his friend, are you not? Don't you want to see him happy?"

Garnette nodded solemnly. "Castic is my bestest friend."

"And you are his. Garnette, the whole village knows how much you mean to him. He loves you, and he would always want you to be happy. To know that the reason you were crying was because of him would make him very sad. You'll hurt his feelings."

Garnette frowned. She fiddled with a string on her dress. "I don't want to make him sad."

"It's okay to be jealous," Leawyn told her gently. "It's how you deal with your jealousy that will define you. Hurting Castic just because he hurt you—something he would never purposely do—isn't right. It's not a fair way to treat someone who loves you."

"He's coming back," Namoriee informed them quietly. They both looked up, seeing Castic heading their way. She glanced down to Garnette. "Do you think you'll be okay?"

Garnette nodded, wiping her face again. Her expression was determined. "Yeah. I won't make him feel bad anymore, even if I do."

"Good." Leawyn untangled herself from Garnette, standing up just as Castic came within distance to them. She stepped back to Namoriee, watching as Castic crouched in front of Garnette.

"Here," Castic panted, thrusting a damp rag to her. She reached for it, giving him a small smile. "Thanks."

Instead of letting her use it, Castic gently began to wipe the tear tracks away from her cheeks.

"You okay now?"

Garnette nodded her head shyly. "I'm sorry Castic. I never meant to ruin your night."

Castic frowned at her, seeming angry.

"Hey," he said firmly, stopping her from looking down by catching her chin. He stared into her eyes, fiercely serious. "You will *never* ruin my day, nor my night. You got it?"

Garnette grinned. "Got it."

"Good," Castic said, tapping her nose. "You hungry?"

She nodded, and Castic helped her stand up, turning his back to her and bending his knees. He tilted his head. "C'mon."

Garnette giggled, hopping on. He hefted her up when he stood, settling her more comfortably on his back before he made his way up the path, giving her a piggyback ride. Garnette waved at them, then laughed when Castic started to run.

Leawyn and Namoriee shared a look, smiling because they both knew.

Even though Castic and Garnette were young...their love story was going to be the most beautiful.

It was well past dark when Leawyn finally crawled into her bed. After the situation with Garnette, Namoriee and she had continued to the dining hut where they had spent a good amount of time. She had watched with great amusement as Namoriee drank more mead than she could handle. The walk to Namoriee's hut was filled with many giggles as she escorted her friend home, leaving as soon as she was safely in bed.

She looked over to the empty side of the bed, missing the heat of her husband's body that always seemed to be warm. Without him here, the bed felt cold and lonely.

She looked around her hut, noticing the subtle differences compared to when she first came to live here. The giant firepit in the middle of the room was unlit, and in the right corner there was a desk that held most of Xavier's things. Two giant chests stood next to each other, holding her and Xavier's clothes separately. Pegs inside of the hut's wall held the plethora of Xavier's weapons, and her bow. She had picked wild flowers and had them scattered around to mask the otherwise manly scent that seemed to be in their hut, and all the other countless knick knacks that she had collect over the course of their marriage.

At the foot of their bed, a slab of wood was slowly taking form in the shape of a crib that Xavier was building. He's been meticulous of every detail as he delicately shaped the wood into a horse. She knew that when he was finished, it would be beautiful. He said that their baby will be strong, and proud. Just like a stallion.

She smiled softly, resting her hand on her stomach. He was convinced that their baby will be a boy, though she was partial to a girl.

She looked over to the empty spot next to her. Sighing heavily, she reached over and blew out the sole candle that she had lit, dousing the room in darkness. She rolled over, turning away from the sight of an empty bedside by closing her eyes. Hoping that sleep will come quickly and without troubles.

It didn't.

XAVIER RETURNED HOME BEFORE TYRONIAN, which wasn't surprising to him in the least. Tyronian often visited their sister-tribe, the Siraces, sometimes spending weeks at a time there. He knew that when he assigned Tyronian and a handful of men to deliver the prisoners to Siraces there was a chance that he would stay awhile. Especially since his dear cousin was trying to avoid a certain girl within their tribe.

He smirked. Popular to his dear wife and cousin's belief, Xavier wasn't as blind to the gossip of his tribe than they thought. He was chief. It was his duty to know every single thing that was happening within his tribe. That included his cousin's infatuation with his wife's handmaiden.

Something must have happened throughout the war, because he caught Tyronian's longing glances he'd send Namoriee every time she's within his eyesight. For some reason or the other, he decided to give the girl space. And because of this, his cousin missed the equally longing looks that Namoriee would send Tyronian when she believed no one was looking.

It was a headache he chose to be ignorant to. But he knew that one day his cousin will come to him to ask permission to claim her as bride–despite the tribulations his decision would create for Tyronian by doing so. But it was his choice, and he knew that he will stand behind his cousin to whichever he decides.

Leawyn is rubbing off on me, he thought wryly.

But his amusement slowly died the closer he got to his hut. His was bone-tired. His muscles ached in multiple paces from his long ride, to and from the lost village. He had dispensed men and slaves to the oceanfront village as soon as he was able to start on the remodel. It is his hope that in a few winters, it will be an functioning second Izayges tribe that Leawyn and him will retire to once their child was old enough to take his place as chief.

But even with his exhaustion, he was dreading to coming home to what undoubtedly will be another long night of Leawyn's screaming. There was once a time that Xavier couldn't wait for the sun to set, so that he and his wife would be alone. It was his favorite part of his day, to be able to love his wife throughout the night. To watch her writhe and scream while he pleasured her to the point of exhaustion. But lately, she was screaming and writhing for a completely different reason.

Her night-terrors were happening more and more frequently, and each morning that she woke, they didn't talk about them. Because she doesn't remember...or she's choosing to ignore them.

He felt helpless, and he hated that feeling. He had given her a chance to tell him what was wrong at the lake, but she had lied to him. It still made him angry. But, instead of punishing her, and demanding her to tell him her deepest, darkest thoughts that he felt belonged to him, he had let her evade his question. It had gone against every fiber of his being. But he was trying to be better. He had made a promise to himself once he had woken up from his deathbed to be a better husband to the woman who had saved him in more ways than one.

He wanted to be the man he knew she wanted him to be, but he was failing.

Even now, knowing that he would undoubtedly walk in to his wife having a nightmare, he wanted her. To slide into her body. To watch his palm make her skin blemish when he spanked her. To bruise her with his hands as he held her down and himself in as deep and as far as he body will allow him to. He wanted to own her.

Her thoughts.

Her body.

Her nightmares.

It was disturbing, how obsessed he was with Leawyn. He wanted to consume every part of her—mind, body, and soul.

It would scare him, if he had any humanity. But he didn't. He didn't even think Leawyn knew how dark he was. How empty.

Until her.

She was the fire that illuminated his surroundings. But if she continued to live this way, he knew that the fire will turn to embers, and eventually burn out.

And if that happened...the would dark devour him. He'd be lost.

He couldn't let that happen.

CHAPTER FIVE

"**S** *TOP!*"

    He froze, his sword still suspended above his head when he made eye-contact with her. He was shocked.

She was terrified.

"Don't make me do it." She was desperate.

He lowered the sword.

"You won't shoot me, Lea."

CHAPTER SIX

XAVIER WAS A LIGHT SLEEPER, years upon years of being on alert forced him to be able to wake on guard with even the slightest of whisper. But it wasn't a whisper that jerked him awake. It was a cry.

Her cry.

He sat up and turned to look at his wife who laid beside him. Tears were streaming down her face, and she was shaking her head. Mumbling in her sleep. He watched her for a moment, conflicted. He should wake her, but he had yet to hear what she said in her night-terrors. Though, he had an idea on what they were about.

He just didn't want to believe it. Selfishly, and filled jealousy, he was in denial.

"No!" she cried. Her face compressed in devastation.

She was going to start screaming soon.

She continued her mumbling, though now it was mixed with half-sobs. He thought he heard his name…but then he also thought she said *his* name.

Bitter, hot, anger filled his veins.

She screamed.

He couldn't take it anymore.

With a growl, he leaned over her.

"Leawyn."

She gasped out a sob, head thrashing.

"Leawyn!" He pinned her down with his body, ignoring how she bucked beneath him. She was trapped, her nightmare no doubt becoming less realistic of the events that she was trapped in.

"Wake up!" he yelled, and with a gasp, she did. Her eyes were wild, still under the power of her fear. Her gaze clashed with his, and slowly, she relaxed. But her eyes were glazed.

"Xavier…" she whispered.

"Yes," he said, his fingers clutching her slim wrists even as they lifted. She traced his rough cheek. He closed his eyes, knowing where her hands will trail down to. Were they always went after she woke from a nightmare.

Her soft palms, clammy and cold, landed on his scar. On the wound that still wasn't healed all the way.

"Don't leave me," she choked.

He opened his eyes and looked down at her. Her eyes glistened like the ocean. It was beautiful, and haunting, and made him feel sad.

"Never," he whispered. "You're mine forever."

He pulled her over his chest, hugging her close as he laid back down.

She was asleep in moments, but he stayed awake until the sun was up; his mind too troubled to rest.

He wasn't sure how much longer he could do this.

Being pregnant was annoying.

"I'm so hungry," Leawyn groaned, laying on her bed. Xavier

paused, shooting her a look from over his shoulder from the spot on the bed he was sitting at.

"You just ate."

Leawyn rolled her eyes. Men.

"Well, considering I have another life inside of my body, forgive me for being hungry more often. I'm quite aware that I just ate, husband. Thank you for pointing out the obvious, but just as well, I'm *still* hungry and I want lamb. Did I *eat* lamb just then?"

It was a rhetorical question, but still her husband opened his dumb mouth. She glared at him, daring him to answer.

He didn't.

"I'll see what I can get you."

"What you'll 'get' me," she sneered, "is lamb."

Xavier was looking at her as if she was a sea monster of legend. But wisely, he continued to keep his mouth shut and got up. She expected him to leave, so she was caught off-guard when he grasped her arms and jerked her to him. Her squeal was cut off when he kissed her until she was nearly breathless.

She blinked, dazed. "What—?"

But she didn't finish. With incredible show of strength, he lifted her so that she was suspended well over his head, her legs draped over his shoulder, and her cunt level with his mouth.

His teeth bit down, moments before his lips wrapped around her flesh and sucked. Hard.

It seemed Xavier wanted to eat before she did.

Her hormones, so primed, it didn't take her very long to orgasm. He continued to devour her, the sounds he was making as he licked and suckled up her juices made her produce more from how intensely erotic it was. Xavier always ate her like she was the elixir for his life, driving her crazy and making her feel so exquisite that her toes curled.

"Xavier, I—" She choked on her words when pure, hot, ecstasy took over her nerve-endings as she climaxed. She was still coming down when Xavier changed their positions, lowering her down his body until the head of his cock notched into her entrance.

Her legs squeezed around his hips when he pushed inside of her.

"Wrap your arms around my neck," he ordered on a grunt, to which she quickly obliged. His fingers into the globes of her ass, and his arms muscles bulged as he started to toss her up and down onto his cock.

It was pure strength, being able to handle her weight so effortlessly. The angle was intense, he was deeper inside of her than she felt he ever had been before. Every thrust—every toss—brushed the most sensitive part of her womanhood, stroking her higher and higher until her eyes rolled back into her head.

"You coming for me, little girl?" Xavier panted, extending his neck to nip hers. She could only manage a whimper, her arms squeezing him tight against her. He chuckled darkly, the sound filled with lust and satisfaction.

"I think you are. Naughty girl. That's twice now you're going to find release without my permission. Think you deserved to be punished, yeah?"

She shook her head adamantly. His form of punishment varies, but he especially liked to bring her on the brink, only to stop her from ever climaxing. She couldn't handle that right now. She was so, so close.

"No, please don't sto—"

Her kissed her, swallowing her moan as she came, shuddering against him. Her release flooded out of her and dripped over his cock that was still embedded inside of her. Her legs unclamped from his waist, leaving Xavier to hold her suspended.

He took a step forward, twisting her in his arms until she was on her hands and knees on their bed.

He gripped her hip with one hand, and dove the other between her legs. She shivered when she felt him brush her slick flesh before delving inside of her. She looked over her shoulder, watching as he used the juices he stole to rub his already slick cock, paying attention to the head.

His eyes met hers, and she swallowed at what she saw.

He leaned over her, kissing her hungrily. It was over before she could think of kissing him back. His grip on her hip changed, became more dominating instead of tender.

"Xavier..." she said uncertainty. He ignored her, his eyes focused on her behind. He brushed a thumb against her puckered hole.

"Who do you belong to?"

"You."

He rewarded her answer by brushing his finger against her again.

"Who owns you?"

She firmed her lips. This was one question she loathed. It earned her a sharp slap on her bottom. She yelped.

"Who owns you?" He enunciated the question with a hard slap to her other cheek.

"You!" She cried, arching her back when he gave two more smacks. "I belong to you."

"That's right," he purred, rubbing the irritated skin of her behind. "You do belong to me, little girl. Now, and until you die. But even in death, I'll find you."

"Xavier," she groaned, when he dipped his thumb into the hole that he had only played with a few times before. Going deeper than he's ever dared.

"Which means this is my body to own and possess," he said, starting to move his thumb in and out of her. "I can do whatever I want to it," he continued, pulling his thumb out only to replace it with his finger. She hissed, her shoulders bunching at the intrusion. "I can take whatever hole you possess that pleases me—and right now I want this one, Leawyn."

Her breaths became unstable, and she could only close her eyes when he reached out to her, yanking her head back by her hair. His lips breathed fire against her ear.

"I'm going to take your virgin asshole, my sweet wife. Stuff my cock inside of that tiny hole until its filled to the brim with my come and you're as filthy as I am. And I'll enjoy every bit of it."

"Oh, Gods," she groaned, falling forward onto her elbows when he released his hold on her. She heard that men sometimes preferred to take women in their ass. She has seen as such, sometimes with the girl withstanding two men inside of her body at once. But she had naively thought that Xavier wouldn't take her in that forbidden place.

She should have known better.

She jerked when he spit, rubbing his saliva onto her untouched territory, and again onto what she could only assumed was his palm. He was making his member as wet as possible for his act. She supposed it was his version of a small mercy.

She tensed when he gripped both her cheeks, spreading them wide open.

"Relax," he murmured. She felt the tip of him against her opening, but he didn't penetrate. Simply rocked against her in mock thrusts.

"Easy for you to say."

He chuckled.

He continued to rock against her, occasionally putting more pressure, but never enough for him to slip in. It was a tactic to get her to relax, and it worked. But she knew the moment he decided he was done, because he aligned himself, and then he was pushing the head of his cock into her body.

It was pure fire, agony. It didn't feel good at all.

She yelped, reaching behind her on instinct but he shackled her wrists behind her back.

"Xavier, I can't," she gasps, tears leaking from the corner of her eyes as he pressed in farther. Gaining another inch. "It hurts!"

"Shh," he soothed. He went deeper. "It will be over soon."

It was a lie. With each inch he eased inside her, she felt like her insides were being burned alive. By the time he finally bottomed out, she was shaking and gasping for breath.

His pelvis was flush against the meat of her bottom, and he stretched over her so that his chest was against his back. He was panting like her, and she could feel the dampness of sweat on his chest.

"You're such a good girl," he whispered against her skin. He peppered kisses against the nape of her neck and the juncture of her collarbone. He continued to whisper praises to her, neither extracting or nor inserting himself more inside of her.

Though the pain never ebbed, it wasn't as sharp as when he first started. That is, until he started to move.

He started off slow, letting her try and get used to the foreign sensation.

"You're so damn tight," Xavier moaned as he withdrew from her body, only thrust back in with more force. Like he couldn't help himself. She groaned.

"You feel so good. So sweet around my cock as your body squeezes it; trying to get rid of it. But I'm not going anywhere. I'm going to keep thrusting into you until your traitorous body remembers that every single bit of it belongs to me. You might be my wife, but your body is my whore. Isn't that right?"

What he was saying was disgusting. Demeaning. More so in the fact that he believed every single word of it. She wanted to fight. To scream her denial. But it would be fruitless. By their way of life, she was his wife and her body *was* his whore—free for him to take either which way he wanted.

Female independence raged at the knowledge, but the darkness of trained lust screamed in acceptance. It was sick pleasure that disgusting words inflicted, which was evidence in the way her nipples puckered. The way she shivered and the way her body relaxed and twisted the pain into pleasure. This act hurt. It didn't feel good, but then it did. She felt too full, and too empty all at once.

"Xavier!" she cried when he thrust hard into her and simultaneously pinched her swollen nub with his fingers.

"That's it, scream for me," Xavier rasped, as he continued to impale himself inside of her. "Let the village hear what a naughty girl you are. I want every man to know that my cock is about to fill your pretty little asshole with my come."

It was the only foreshadowing he gave her, because in the next moment he gripped both her hips and started to ram his cock furiously inside of her ass until his skin was slapping against her own, and her breasts swayed with each violent jerk.

Soon, her elbows couldn't support her weight and Xavier followed her down as she collapsed forward, the fur blankets privy to her screams and moans.

Xavier was groaning from above her, and she knew he was close when he started to curse her name and how good she felt.

"Shit," he grunted, and then he stilled above her and she felt him jet inside of her.

He held her to him for long moments, then slowly peeled himself off her. She whimpered when his softening member slipped free from her body.

"So damn beautiful," he growled. She couldn't see him, but she knew he was looking at the evidence of his release. Gentle fingers spread her cheeks apart, and she squeezed her eyes shut in embarrassment. The slow trickle down her crack made her shift restlessly. His whispered approval did nothing to lessen her mortification and she was relieved when he finally stood.

She heard him move, and then his fingers were rubbing against her lips. Her eyes peeled open, colliding with his lust-filled ones.

"Say it," he ordered in a rasp. Her brows furrowed, confused at the glimpse of anxiety she caught in his gaze. His expression shuttered, and the energy around him changed.

"Say it, Leawyn."

"I love you."

Her confusion only grew when his body relaxed, and he let out a sigh that could pass as relieved. He picked her up gingerly, settling himself inside of their bed. He didn't offer to clean her up from his release, and she knew that in a sick way he found pleasure in her having it on her skin. He pulled her against her chest and ordered her to sleep.

She listened.

XAVIER WATCHED LEAWYN SLEEP. SHE had been quick to slumber, his body having exhausted hers. He knew that she was going to be sore tomorrow, and the knowledge both pleased and disgusted him.

He had warned her before that he would claim her ass one day. It was foolish to think otherwise. His need for his wife was never sated. He could never get enough of her. It was a fact, but...

He lost control.

His obsession and his insane lust for Leawyn took over his mind, until all he could think about was owning her again. The beast inside of him was released from its cage and it devoured it's prey.

It was only until her metaphorical blood was dripping down it's teeth did the haze lift, and he realized what he had done. This act of lovemaking was painful. He knew that. He jad planned to to train Leawyn to enjoy it, to trick her body into accepting the feeling of him inside her. To have her lean that though anal could cause pain at first, it could and will eventually lead to a different, special kind of pleasure.

He was supposed to ease her into it. To go slow. *Gentle.*

He lifted the covers from off her body, turning her so that her bottom was bared to his gaze once again. He could see the stain of his come, the redness on the pale flesh from his palm.

When he had stood in front of her, and seen what she looked

like…he knew he had done the thing he promise he would never do again.

Fear captured his heart, squeezed his lungs when she didn't answer him right away. The pressure only eased when she finally uttered the words he needed to hear as desperately as he needed to breathe.

He released the blankets and turned his gaze away.

Never again, he promised himself.

But he knew it was a lie.

CHAPTER SEVEN

"I CAN'T LET YOU KILL HIM."

     "Everything will be okay, Lea. I'm going to take care of you."

     "You killed innocent people."

"They didn't belong."

"Do I not belong?"

"Of course, you belong, Lea."

Relief. She felt relief.

Until she didn't.

"We'll rule our people together."

Numb.

She shook her head, felt the tear slip down her cheek.

CHAPTER EIGHT

SHE WAS SORE FOR DAYS.

The reasoning for her soreness was mortifying, even if it the memory made her hot. Xavier had taken mercy on her and has not tried to make love to her in *that* way for the last few weeks. In fact, his lovemaking had changed completely. It was like he was a different person, because he never demanded. Never exuded force. When they would have sex, it would be almost virginal. She couldn't understand it.

That was not like Xavier.

But she couldn't deny that she was grateful in part for the small respite, because she didn't think she would ever be ready for him to take her like the animals do again. Between her pregnancy sickness, and sex-induced-sickness, she had severely lacked in her duties as lady chief. So when she was finally able to get out of bed without wincing with each step, she started her day. First, she checked on the horses and livestock, as well as met with Aggod, the village healer, to ask for some herbs that helped ease fatigue. She was delayed when she had to settle a civic dispute, and break up a fight between two brothers fighting over the same girl. Which settled when said girl offered herself up to them both.

At the same time.

She shook her head with a wry smile. Sometimes, she swore that she was living in the Siraces village—where that kind of union was more commonplace—instead of the Izayges. Upon reaching the market square, Leawyn made a point to visit every merchant. The tradition started when Namoriee had dragged her out here early into her marriage. She had told her how there hadn't been a lady chief of the Izayges for a long time, and that her village people were desperate to know her, if not a bit untrusting.

She made it her mission after that to try and know every single one of the people inhabiting her large tribe and gain their trust individually.

She smiled at Tutor, the old clay maker and one of her favorite merchants to talk to.

"You're looking well today, Tu. Your wife must be taking good care of you."

Tutor, whose hair would have been white had he not shaved it all off, waved a hand that was wrinkled and hardworking at her.

"Bah!" he spat. "Old bat won't leave me alone, she will."

Said old bat, whacked him with a damp cloth, scowling down at him. "Ya don't die!" Yinna exclaimed. "Drop dead and maybe I will, eh?"

Tutor glowered, looking every bit displeased and grouchy, but he couldn't hide his fondness for Yinna if his life depended on it. She shook her head in amusement, placing payment in one of the clay pots crafted.

"Oh no yer don't, Lady Chief!" Yinna yelled after her, trying scoop up her payment and catch up to her already walking form. "Ya always be placing payment without a purchase. I will not be having it!"

"Goodbye, you two. See you again in a week!" Leawyn laughed. She ignored as they tried to argue with her, but then ended up arguing with themselves. Yinna and Tutor had a good business. Clay pots and jugs were wildly important, but she knew that Tutor's hands have started to ache him more than he could start to handle. She couldn't stand the thought of him pushing through his joint pain more than he had to.

Xavier and Leawyn usually didn't have to buy or want for anything. But she didn't want to be the kind of lady chief that just took from her people, without giving anything back. Which is why she always made a point to pay for services that she didn't render.

Strong arms wrapped around her waist, and before she could react, they lifted her up in a hug, squeezing her half to death.

"Beautiful! When are you going to leave your husband and come to me, eh?"

"Tyronian, welcome back!" Leawyn beamed once she was back on her feet, shading her eyes from the sun with her hand. "How was the Siraces?"

Tyronian, her only fellow tribesmen who shared her blonde hair, shrugged. "It was well. They weren't attacked like we were so nothing much has changed upon their return."

Leawyn made a sound of acknowledgement, studying him. It had been a few weeks since she had last seen him. Although he greeted her in the same cheeky way he always did, he looked troubled. His lips that were usually easily pulled back into a smile were downturned, and his eyes held a sadness that she didn't like.

She rested her hand on his forearm, quietly requesting his attention. He was scanning the village-port, which was always the hubbub of activity in the Izayges.

"Why do you torture yourself so," she asked quietly. "Why don't you just claim her?"

Want flashed in his blue-orbs before they settled desolately. "I made a promise," he answered quietly, almost to himself.

He stepped back from her with a fake smile. "It was good to see you cousin. You grow more beautiful as your baby does."

Automatically, her hands rested on her stomach and the bump that her dress hid.

"Shh!" she hissed, scanning their surroundings to make sure no one heard him. Xavier and she weren't ready for the tribe to know yet. *Well,* she thought. *At least I'm not.*

Something that made Xavier very displeased. He had wanted to announce her pregnancy as soon as he recovered.

Tyronian laughed, walking backwards. "Until we meet again, beautiful." And with a wink, he was gone.

She shook her head, turning around to finish her shopping, when a flash of movement across the way caught her eye. She stared, trying to convince herself that the person she was seeing wasn't there.

It wasn't possible, it shouldn't be.

Because that person was dead.

She stumbled backward, her heart beating so forcefully, she was having difficulty drawing breath. She stared as blood started to stain the shirt her ghost was wearing, trickling in a spiral and expanding.

"You're not real," she whispered in horror. She clenched her eyes shut when the figure started to walk towards her. "You're not *real!*"

She opened her eyes and jerked when they collided with the ones that used to be alive. They were standing face to face.

"*Lea.*"

She whimpered. She felt something on her palms, and when she looked down at them, they were covered in red.

Blood.

She screamed.

If Xavier had the ability to wonder anything passed his concern right now, it would be how the boy Castic always seemed to be the one to collect him when there was trouble. How the boy seemed to always be in the right place at the right time was boggling to him. He supposed that he should be thankful. After all, if it wasn't for him practically barreling into him, panting and panicking, he wouldn't have known where to find his wife who seemed to be having breakdown in the middle of market square.

His villagers gave him a wide-berth as he made his way through, their gazes concerned and locked on Leawyn, who had curled into herself, rocking back and forth. He hesitated, caught off guard by the sight. He pushed forward until he was crouched in front of her.

"Leawyn?"

It was as if she didn't hear him. He moved the hair away from her face, his brows drawing together at the vacant glaze to her blue irises.

"What happened?" he barked at no one in particular. But of course, Castic was the only one brave enough to step forward.

"She just started screaming, Chief. I was helping my momma and I thought she was going to ask me to come over because she was looking right at me." Xavier followed the direction to which Castic was pointing, noticing the fabric merchant stand that his mother, Jsaya, ran. Once Leawyn learned that Jsaya was Castic's mother, she made a point to always purchase fabrics from her. He turned back to Castic.

"Then what happened? Did she say anything?"

Castic shook his head, looking distressed. "I went to her, I tried to ask. But she just kept screaming. Said blood was on her hands, but I didn't see a cut."

Xavier shook his head. Blame laid heavy on his shoulders. He was about to scoop her up in his arms when their eyes locked. It stopped him cold.

There's only two instances that can put that kind of void in someone's eyes. And Leawyn was two for two.

"Help me."

The whisper was pure hopelessness.

He stood up with her in his arms, cradling her close. She ignored everyone standing watch by turning her face toward his chest, and his gaze alone warned of them of what should happen if he were to hear any whispers about her behind their back about this. He began his march back to their hut, and when the sky split open with thunder, and the rain drove down from above, he thought it was fitting.

Because he was done giving Leawyn time to entrust him with her secrets. To do it her way. He was going to be getting the answers he sought.

Even if he had to follow her into the dark and drag her out of it kicking and screaming.

CHAPTER NINE

SOUND.

So many different sounds.

"Don't make me do it."

Metal hitting metal, screams of triumph, and pain. There were parts of the field that were on fire; it caused heat to blaze across her face, seeming to boil the tears streaming down her cheeks.

"You won't shoot me, Lea."

Smoke.

She wished that was the reason for her tears. It would make the betrayal she was feeling easier to hide.

The hurt.

"We can rule our people together."

Hope.

Conviction.

She knew what she had to do.

Anguish.

"These are not my people."

The arrow left her fingers.

Sound…it was so versatile.

The sound of her arrow burrowing inside of flesh and bone would be one she'll never forget.

CHAPTER TEN

HER SILENCE WAS DRIVING HIM mad.

His wife, who usually was so quick to retort or make her presence known, was silent. She hadn't spoken a word to him since she asked him to help her. Hadn't uttered a sound as he carried her through the rain and mud back to their hut. Nor when he had stripped her out of her wet clothes and changed her into dry ones. She hasn't spoke or moved after he placed her on the bed.

Or when the storm clouds traded with inky blackness of night.

He had distanced himself, staring at her from across the room. Her small frame was huddled atop their bed, her dainty feet bare on the floor. The slip he had changed her into was too big for her frame, it dipped down and exposed her shoulder. His gaze trailed down her back, to her long hair that shined like gold and fluttered in the firelight like birdwings.

His pretty, broken little bird.

He was going to make her sing.

He didn't bother to muffle his steps, so he knew she heard him coming for her. She didn't move when he brushed his hand down her slim back. His hand curved, trailing upward until it grasped her neck. He felt her pulse against his fingertips, reveling in the steady rhythm. He flexed, pressing into the delicate skin.

It was a warning.

And like the docile pet she was, she heeled to the unspoken command.

She broke.

"I'm a killer," she choked. "I killed him, *me*, and that's something I'll have to live with for the rest of my life….and I don't know how." She looked up at him, and even when her eyes sparkled with tears and gut-wrenching anguish, she was still the most beautiful woman he's ever seen.

"Leawyn," he rumbled. Covetous and angry, because he knew which *he* she was speaking of. He had banned the name from every leaving her pretty lips.

"Everytime I close my eyes, I see him."

Her voice was no more than a whisper, but he heard it as if she shouted it. He tensed, irrational jealousy coursing through his veins and making his blood hot, but the haunting pain in the words made his cold heart ache.

"I feel the bow in my hands. Hear the tautness of the string… feel the fletching leave my fingers." She was facing him, but her gaze was dazed, staring sightlessly over his shoulder.

"It haunts me, Xavier."

"You saved my life." He crouched in front of her. His fingers left indents in her chin when he held it hostage. "Are you saying you regret that?"

Her expression crumbled.

"No," she whispered, her voice cracking. "I'd lie, steal, cheat, and kill for you. I'll do anything for you, Xavier. And that *terrifies* me."

She focused on him, her beautiful blue eyes a pool of tears she didn't let fall.

"What kind of person does that make me?"

"Strong," he hissed. His grip left her chin to trade up for her hair. Holding it tight in his fist, he tilted her head back and forced her to look at him when he went nose to nose with her. "A survivor, a protector, a *warrior*, a—"

"A killer."

He couldn't stand it any longer. Suddenly, he knew what he had to do.

With a snarl, he stood, bringing her up with him. He ignored her cry when he used his grip on her hair to drag her outside with him.

"Xavier, stop!" She yelped, stumbling, having trouble finding her footing in the mud. She gripped his wrist, trying to pry his hands out of her hair. He hasn't treated her this way since the beginning of their marriage.

But he didn't let go, and he didn't stop.

When their destination became apparent, she tried to dig in her heels, her face ashen.

"No." She started to fight him again. "No! Please, no!"

There were two guards stationed in front. "Give me your bow," he barked, snatching it up with one hand when they quickly complied. The other opened the door.

They stalked inside, Leawyn crying and begging him as they went. The door slammed shut behind them when he launched her forward, making her fall onto her hands and knees.

There were twenty prisoners, some healthier than others.

He grabbed one by the neck at random, dragged him forward and forced him onto his knees in front of Leawyn.

He tossed the bow so that it landed directly in front of her. He held out an arrow.

"Kill him."

She sucked in a sharp breath. "What?"

He tilted his head down to the prisoner he still held in his grasp. "Kill him." It was an order.

She shook her head. "No." She pushed herself up hastily so that she sat back on her heels.

"No!"

He regarded her coolly. "Why not? You're a killer, aren't you?" He mocked, his lips quirking—but it wasn't even close to a smile. He held out the arrow again.

"Take it."

"Xavier…" she whimpered. "Please don't do this." His features twisted, a snarl on his lips.

"Take it!" He bellowed.

Her breaths were choppy, and her shoulders heaved.

But he didn't care.

He couldn't.

"Now," he said calmly, standing taller once she finally did what he bid. "Pick up the bow and notch the arrow."

"Xavier—"

"Now, Leawyn."

"No!" She sobbed, shaking uncontrollably.

"You're a killer!" He yelled, his voice carrying over her cries. "You said so yourself, so this should be easy for you. You'll do anything for me, right? Then, grab your bow, and kill him. Do it!"

She didn't move.

He jerked the prisoner forward, staring her in the eyes cruelly. "Pick up that bow, right now. I won't ask you again." His threat was clear.

She coughed, trying to find her breath from her sobbing. Picking up the bow, she notched it unsteadily. He easily contained the prisoners struggles, who now plead for his life. He yanked the prisoner's head back by his hair, baring his throat.

"You see *him*, don't you?" Xavier said, his voice deceptively light. "You look at this scum—who helped in the destruction of your tribe, who lifted a blade to our people, who's kin killed everything, and everyone you've ever loved— but all you see is *him!*" He spat, disgusted.

"Please, Xavier," she choked. "Stop."

"He deserved to die, Leawyn." He screamed at her, pushing her boundaries in more ways than one. "Just like this one does." He urged the prisoner closer.

"He is the enemy. You're the lady chief of this tribe, and my *wife*," he growled, full of menace and meaning. "And I am *ordering* you to kill him."

The bow was shaking in her hands as she looked at the prisoner, stared into his eyes.

Then he saw it.

The waver in Leawyn, the weakness, the uncertainty.

The moral consciousness.

The lightness.

With a cry, she lowered the bow, dropping it and scrambling back from it like it was a demon. "I can't do it," she said, broken. "I can't kill him."

Without pause, Xavier yanked the dagger from his hip, and before Leawyn could stop him, he slit his captive's throat. She screamed, flinching when his blood splattered across her face but Xavier didn't care. He let the body go, and it dropped, flapping around like a fish, before it stilled laying in a pool of blood.

He crouched in front of her, moved a red-tipped strand of hair away from her forehead. He waited for her gaze to meet his, and when they did, they were wide and red-rimmed.

Shocked.

Destroyed.

Scared.

He lifted his hand that was coated in blood so that it hovered between them.

"You're not the killer, Leawyn," he told her quietly. "I am."

CHAPTER ELEVEN

L EAWYN STARED AT THE DOOR. The wood was thick, matching the hut it served as the blockade to what was within. It's been days.

They haven't looked at each other, haven't spoken.

And she couldn't help but thinking it was her fault.

She thought back to that night. The look on his face when he had spoken his truth…his eyes.

He had left her there, with the man he killed. She had started at the lifeless eyes of the man until his blood soaked her dress. She couldn't move.

She couldn't escape.

He left her to deal with her demons. It wasn't until the next morning that he had come to collect her, staring down at her with the same dead eyes that his victim had. She remembered how her legs were numb from staying in the same position for too long. But Xavier didn't help her up; her lesson wasn't over.

He escorted her to the lake, handed her a new dress, and left her alone to wash.

And that was it.

He hasn't looked at her in the eyes since.

She closed her eyes, inhaling deep through her nose. When her fingers gripped the handle, her eyes opened.

She faced her demons.

She yanked open the door and went inside.

It was time for him to face his.

HE WAS NOSE-DEEP INTO THE map of land Tyronian had delivered to him this morning, and he hasn't been able to come up since. His eyes scanned the vast landscape, the markings of cliffs and ocean, trying to plot the best course of action to bring his vision to life, when his door opened.

He gave explicit orders for him not to be disturbed. He looked up with a snarl, ready to condemn the person who dared to disobey but it died when he caught sight of Leawyn who's back was turned from him as she closed the door.

She turned around to face him, staring at him head-on.

The sound of the lock sliding into place was loud and the air fizzled with the tension that always seemed to follow them.

She didn't speak, and neither did he while he watched her come to him. When she was right in from of him—scarce inches separating their bodies from touching—she went to her knees and reached for his belt. His gaze grew heated, his abs going taunt when she undid the buckle and peeled back the fabric to reveal his cock that was already half-hard.

"What do you think you're doing, little girl?" He asked huskily. It was the first time he's spoken to her since that night. His hand snaked through her soft locks before fisting them at her nape.

"Shh."

And before he could retort, she put the head of his engorged flesh into her mouth and sucked.

Hard.

He hissed, his thighs bunching from the pleasure. She went at him firm, sucking him just like he taught her how. Taking him in long strokes and deep into her mouth until she gagged his meaty flesh.

Gods, he loved that sound.

His eyes closed, his head tipping back. He was lost in what she was doing and how she was making him feel. Her right hand gripped his shaft, sliding up and down with a firm grip while she licked the tip, her tongue swirling and lapping up the tears his dick wept in appreciation.

His grip tightened in her hair. His hips jerked, wanting to pump into her mouth with the same intensity that he would with her tight warmth, but he held himself back. Before, he would have no problem taking control. He wouldn't hesitate to hold her head still while he choked her with his cock, slamming it deep into her mouth. He'd make her take him until he came on down her throat, forcing her to swallow every last drop. Then, he would pick her up and bend her over his desk and pound into her until she was screaming.

But that was the old Xavier, one he had already let slip. He promised that he would be better. That he wouldn't hurt her...or their baby. He already failed thrice—he wasn't going to do it a fourth.

An emotion clogged his throat, so suddenly, it startled him. It was fighting with his pleasure, causing his body to fight in this weird battle on which one would prevail.

"Leawyn," he choked. He wanted her to stop. He wanted to pull her closer.

The decision was made for him, because at that moment, her left hand cupped his sac the same moment she tugged his hips to her, taking his entire length into her mouth until her chin brushed against him. It was the move he had done to her multiple times, one he taught her to enjoy.

With a mix between a growl and a quiet cry, his release jetted into her waiting and willing throat. He groaned, holding her head to him a moment before he pulled back. She looked up at him with hungry eyes when his partially flaccid cock slipped free from her mouth. She must have seen something in his expression, because hers became almost desperate.

"Xavier," she whispered, her tone raw. "Please."

CHAPTER TWELVE

H E WASN'T GOING TO DO IT.

She wanted to cry. It's been days since he's last touched her, ever since the night she refused to kill the prisoner.

It was the longest he's ever gone.

Even when she was broken and bruised—and he knew she wanted nothing to do with him—he had taken her. He played her body like it was an instrument until she craved his touch. His rawness.

His demands.

He made sure he was the master of her body, trained only to serve and want him.

She needed him...so why didn't he want her?

"Leawyn." He tried to pull away from her, but she wouldn't let him.

"Did I not please you?"

His eyes flared with heat, easing some of her concern. "You

did," he said, stroking her cheek until his thumb could press against her bottom lip that was still glistening from her act.

"Very much so."

"Then why won't you take me?"

Conflict reflected in his gaze before he masked it. His hand dropped from her face.

"Leawyn…" he sighed.

She became angry when he tried to pull away from her again. She stood, using the hand he gave to help her up to slide it down her body and between her thighs. He sucked in a sharp breath.

"You feel that?" she demanded, keeping her grip tight. His fingers, as if they couldn't help themselves, twitched against her wetness. "Answer me."

His nostrils flared at her tone, but he didn't shy away from her gaze. "Yes."

She forced his hand to stroke her from palm to tip. Pleasure flared within her. She was so painstakingly hot for him that even the slightest touch of his shot fire within her womb.

"*You* did this to me," she growled, practically humping his hand now. His breathing grew heavy, his eyes shooting from watching her gyrate and back up to her eyes. Like he couldn't decide where to look.

"You haven't touched me, and I'm *dying*, Xavier. I want you, I want your cock inside me, owning me. Do you not want the same?"

"You know I do," he growled, anger distorting his features. "Don't speak such foolish things, Leawyn. It's beneath you."

"Then why won't you *touch me*!" She snarled. He looked away, but she still caught the shame he tried to hide. It was like a slap in the face.

"Fine," she said, trying to hide the fact that she was dangerously close to tears. She brought his hand from out of her skirts, flinging it away. "If you don't want me, I'll find someone who will."

She turned, barely managed to make two steps before she was hauled back against him roughly. Her back collided with his chest, and she choked when his hand went around her throat, the other banded across her chest. She felt the heat of his breath against the shell of her ear before he spoke.

"You will do no such thing."

"Why?" She challenged. "You clearly don't want me anymore. Why shouldn't I enjoy the touch of another?"

"I'll kill any man who touches you," he snarled, pure wrath in his tone. "You're mine, Leawyn. Always and forever."

A frisson ran over her, and she couldn't help the crack in her voice. "Then why don't you want me anymore?"

She felt him stiffen, and then he was turning her around to face him. She stubbornly met his eyes, refusing to be ashamed of her tears. He searched her face, lingering on her tears. The storm in his expression eased. His enormous hands cupped her face.

"Why would you say such a ridiculous thing?"

"Is it?" she countered, sniffing. "You haven't touched me. You avoid me. Was it because I was weak? Did I disgust you so much?

"Leawyn," he sighed, bending so that their foreheads touched. He looked tortured. "You are still, and ever will be, the most beautiful flower." He pulled back to look at her, his eyes suspiciously red-rimmed. It instantly made her tears refill.

"I failed you," he said, voice raw. "I promised myself that I would be better. Treat you like you deserved, and then what I did..." he swallowed audibly. "I don't want to hurt you anymore, but it's all I'm capable of doing. And the worst is that, sometimes, I *do* want to hurt you. I don't know how to be gentle."

"Xavier," she guides his face back to hers when he looked away, like he was unable to face his weakness. She moved on her tiptoes, so that their mouths was more level. "I fell in love with you...just the way you are. Yes, change was required, but that was so that we could *grow*. I don't want you to change who you are."

"But, Leawyn—"

She yanked him down while she surged up, slamming their lips together in a hungry kiss. He resisted, then groaned, hauling her closer to him. Her breasts cushioned his chest, and she whimpered when he gripped her hair, taking control of the kiss. It was sloppy, and wet, their tongues battling. They were both gasping when she broke apart from him.

"I don't want gentle," she whispered huskily, gripping his neck to keep him close. Their noses were touching, their gaze locked. She reveled in the battle in his gaze.

The fire.

The want, and the need.

"Sometimes, I want it rough. Don't change," she panted, trying to bring him closer. Her hips gyrated, the pulsing need making the friction electric. "I want you. Right now, right here. Own me."

With each word, his gaze grew heavier, headier, with his lust, until by the end—he snapped.

A savage growl escaped his lips when he lifted her off her feet. Her legs wrapped around his waist. Taking one step, Xavier swiped the top of his desk—uncaring that everything crashed to the floor—and laid her down.

Gaze going somnolent, she watched him push her dress until it bunched around her thighs, standing between them. He stole a hard kiss from her lips before stretching over her, his lips at her ear.

"You're mine," he growled, and then he was inside her in one hard surge.

She groaned at the familiar stretch. No matter how many times he's taken her, it amazed her at how it felt— a pinch of pain, and erotic pleasure. How his cock straddled the line of too big, and just enough; it was divine. It drove her insane with lust and need and made her hopeless but to hold onto him, nails raking down his back as he set a punishing pace.

Their flesh slapped together, reverberating around them. The table rocked, the wood groaning but she was so overcome with desire that was rapidly lighting her insides on fire to worry about it breaking.

She knew Xavier would catch her if it did. He'll always catch her.

"I love how tight you are," he groaned, a fine sheen of sweat making his chest muscles glisten. She wanted to lick it all up. "I keep trying to stretch you with my cock, but your body is too greedy. Can you feel how it squeezes around me, milking it with your juices like it never wants to let me go?"

As if to punctuate his point, he drove hard into her, then pulled out slow, his gaze on their joining body parts.

"Look at it," he whispered, grabbing hold of her hair and angling her head down. Forcing her to watch.

And Gods and Goddess, it was so erotic.

She watched his meaty length plunge into her in sure strokes, coming away wet. She trembled, heat rippling through her and curling her toes.

"I want you to watch," he rasped, picking up speed. "I want you to watch as your come floods out of you and soaks my cock."

"Xavier," she whimpered. His words, the feel of him inside of her, watching him own her...it was too much. She came, calling out his name as she spiraled out of control and tossed into absolute bliss.

"Don't you dare close your eyes." He ordered, stilling inside of her. "Open them."

She listened. Lids heavy, she looked down. Xavier pulled out of her, and she could clearly see her essence blanketing him. She shivered.

"Your gaze leaves again, and your ass gets spanked."

It was so tempting to disobey him, but she did as she was told and continued to watch him plow into her body. No longer caring about dragging it out, Xavier plowed into her.

Hard.

Fast.

Deep.

Driving her to the point of pain, but it was the sweetest of pain.

Her second orgasm came quick, leaving her gasping and shaking in his arms. His heavy sack slapped against her so continuously it sounded like one beat. His grip on her hair grew even more tight, making tears sting her eyes, but she couldn't help how her body started to convulse around him in orgasm while he chased his own. He thrust into her a few more times until with a grunt, he pulled out of her, and she watched his come jet over her glistening folds and part of her stomach. His grip left her hair with a heavy exhale and he stepped back. His gaze trailed down her body, resting on where his fluid was still on her.

"Beautiful," he murmured.

He gathered his come covering her pink lips and brought them to her mouth. Her lips parted willingly, and he pressed them inside, her tongue automatically swirling around the digits and sucked. He watched her, his arousal at the dirtiness apparent in both his eyes and his body. He gathered his come on her skin two more times, until her mound was clean, but her stomach wasn't. Once satisfied, he pulled away, growling when she nipped the calloused pads. He stepped back, surveying her body.

"Look at how beautiful you are," he whispered, sounding like gravel. "Spread out on my table, flushed and soaking wet. Spread your legs. Wider."

She compiled, her chest heaving, until she was completely bare to his gaze. She felt the wetness pool out of her. His nostrils flared at the sight, watching its journey. He didn't look at her when he commanded his next order.

"Touch yourself."

She balanced her weight on one elbow, trailing a shaking hand down her navel until her pointer and middle finger touched her clitoris. Her head dipped back as she started a steady strum, rolling the slick bud around in circles.

Xavier didn't move.

He didn't touch her, but his stare felt physical. He was completely focused on her movements, commanding her every so often until her thighs started to shake, her movements became frantic.

She was going to come.

"Don't you dare," Xavier said, now in front of her. "Beg me."

"Please," she gasped, full on trembling now. "Please, may I come?"

His smile was evil. "No."

He slapped her hand away, and she screeched. In one fluid motion, he went to his knees, grabbed her, tugged until her bottom was dangling off the table, and bent his head. He sucked her throbbing nub into his mouth, and bit down.

Every single nerve in her body combusted.

The bliss traveled through her blood, heating it, making it boil and bubble. She swore the world went silent. Her ears rung, her body stiffened, and she screamed without making a sound. When she came down, Xavier was still between her legs, lapping up her juices like it was his favorite meal.

Her hands—trembling uncontrollably—buried into his long hair, gripped it tight. She took control then, and he let her. She rolled her hips, making love to his face in fast, uncoordinated jerks until she was once again lost in the ocean of euphoria.

She sagged against the table, too weak to hold herself up anymore. He gave her mound one, sweet kiss, then rose, bending over her and giving her lips the same so that she could taste herself.

They didn't speak for a while, both trying to catch their breaths. Something changed with them, something vital sliding in place. Surprisingly, Xavier was the one to break their silence.

"You're the only one I will ever love, Leawyn. I don't know how, or why, but you chose me, even when I forced you into a life you never wanted. I'm a monster, who tried to be in sheep's clothing because I thought that's what you wanted. I was trying to make up for my past, but I think I always knew it wouldn't be possible. I was..." he struggled, and her heart broke a little bit.

He was trying to be someone he wasn't. Someone he thought

she wanted. Every single fiber of Xavier's being was dominant. A cold warrior that didn't know any other weakness except death.

It was all he knew, until her.

She hugged him, and he stiffened—like he always did when confronted with affection—then relaxed. She couldn't speak right away, too emotional. She partly blamed the baby with how extreme he/she was making her.

"I think we need to forget the past. We need to bury it. Kill it, if we must. Our beginning will not define our future from here on out." She pulled back to look at him, finding him already staring at her. "From now on, no more secrets. No more lies. We bare our souls, Xavier. No matter how broken they are."

He closed his eyes, his forehead meeting hers. "I can't promise you that I will be any better than how I was. You drive me mad, Leawyn. My need is obsessive, never sated. I want to break you, to clip your wings and watch you try to fly. I'm messed up. Something in me died long ago, and the only bit of humanity I have left was revived by you. But it's a corpse. A hollow shell of what I could have been under different circumstances."

She smiled, stroking his cheek. His hair. His scars.

"I'll be everything you're not. You might have clipped my wings, but they grow back. Every time. You'll never be able to take that from me. I'll be your humanity, Xavier." She brought his hand to rest on her stomach, and the baby bump that grew each day. "As will our children. You'll be no one's monster, but my own."

He said nothing in response, but she knew that he accepted what she was telling him. He wasn't going to try and be someone he wasn't anymore. Because it was a painful truth that Xavier could never be the husband she had dreamed of as a girl. But he can, however, be a warrior. Conquering his most trying war for the rest of his life.

Their love.

CHAPTER THIRTEEN

T<small>HERE WAS NOTHING MORE THAT</small> Xillik hated than being interrupted—even worse when he happened to be balls deep in a woman who was screaming his name at the time. But that's exactly what happened.

By his annoying twin brothers, no less.

"Rhoxon, Ryder, get out!" he hollered at them. Not that he was bothered by modesty—but it wasn't him he was worried about.

Ryder—the less annoying one—blinked dumbly at him while Rhoxon sucked in a breath. Both of them stared at the girl underneath him, who looked like she desperately wanted to disappear. She buried her face into his chest, trying uselessly to hide.

"Shit. Isn't that...?" Rhoxon breathed.

"Yup," Ryder nodded, still staring.

"Oh man. He's gonna be so mad."

"Really mad," Ryder quipped.

"Xi, brother, what were you thinking?"

"I'm thinking that I'm going to kill you both if you don't get out!"

Rhoxon's brows lifted sky-high. "I think you're the one who should be worried about being killed, bro."

Ryder snickered.

He growled, beyond frustrated. He didn't know why the Gods felt like they had to curse him with twin brothers. They were incorrigible.

"What do you want? As you can see, I'm busy."

"Oh, we can see alright," Rhoxon and Ryder said simultaneously with identical grins.

"Please," a soft voice said, her tone drowning in mortification and shame.

They turned their attention to her, who still had her face pressed against his skin. The twin's expression lost their teasing, and they looked to him.

"We'll leave, give you a minute," Rhoxon said.

"A short one," Ryder added.

"Because of her. But—"

"Hurry." They finished together.

Xillik was so used to the twins finishing each other's sentences it hardly fazed him anymore.

Didn't make it any less annoying though.

He sighed, running a frustrated hand through his hair. "What's so important?"

The twins looked at each other, then back at him.

"Mother and father are here," they informed him simultaneously.

Nothing softened his cock more than that sentence.

"Shit."

"MOTHER. YOU LOOK WELL."

At the sound of his voice, his mother turned, a huge smile on her face. "Xillik!" Leawyn beamed, cupping his cheek after accepting his kiss once he reached her. "You look as handsome as ever. Almost as handsome as your father was."

Xillik rolled his eyes, smiling good-naturedly.

"And you're as beautiful as I remember you to be, mother."

It was true. His mother had aged well, and she was still as vibrant as he remembered her to be when he was a child. She was still petite, with laugh lines that crinkled her eyes when she smiled, and hair that, though still blonde, was streaked with white. Older, but nevertheless beautiful.

"Oy! What about us?" The twins exclaimed, ambling up behind them with Hunter, their youngest brother.

Xillik, the twins, and Hunter all inherited their mother's blonde hair, and they all had their father's eyes, except for Xillik. They were all similarly built, with Xillik being the tallest, standing close to six-foot-seven, while his brothers ranged from six-foot-five to six-foot-three. They all had broad shoulders, and trim waists, though the twins were the bulkiest.

While they looked similar, their personalities couldn't have been more different. Xillik, trained to take over the tribe at a young age, was the most serious, carrying the weight of his people's wellbeing on his shoulders. The twins were trouble makers, and rarely somber. Out of all the siblings, they were the ones who were in trouble the most growing up, with their cousin Tyberious. Hunter was quiet, but outgoing. His smile was easy, and his eyes were warm.

While his mother fussed over his brothers, Xillik looked around, and frowned when he realized two important people were missing.

"Where's father and Lévaunia?"

At his question, his brothers looked around them, coming to the same realization.

"Yeah, where is our sister?" Ryder asked, smiling. "I've missed her."

"More like you miss someone to fall for your tricks," Hunter joked.

"Hey, it's not *our* fault she's gullible," Rhoxon and Ryder said together.

Xillik kept his attention on his mother, not liking the look she wore.

"Mother," he said suspiciously, gaze narrowed. "What's that look for?"

"Hmm? What look?" she replied, trying—and failing—to appear innocent. Like a pack of wolves who sensed prey, they pressed in.

"Where is she?" He asked again.

Leawyn's gaze flitted from them nervously, before she scowled, throwing her hands in the air.

"Honestly boys," she huffed exasperatedly. "You think I'm scared of you all?"

"Hmm, y'know what I think?" Rhoxon said.

"What's that Rhox?" Ryder replied.

"I think that our dear old mother doesn't *want* to tell us where our little sister is."

"Huh, I think you're right Rhox!" Ryder nodded. "Why do you think that is?"

"Well," Rhoxon mused, "I think it's because she knows that we—being Lévaunia's caring older brothers—won't like what dear old sis is doing."

Leawyn huffed while Hunter was openly snickering now, and even Xillik had to grin at their antics.

"Give it up, mother," Xillik said, humor lacing his words. "You've been outed."

Leawyn, for her credit, didn't even flinch. "I will do no such thing," she sniffed.

Rhoxon made a big show about cracking his knuckles. "I was hoping it wouldn't have to come to this."

"Don't you dare," she warned, backing up a step. She leveled the twins with a look, who just smiled evilly at her. "I mean it!"

As usual, they didn't listen and with a screech from his mother, they pounced. Xillik was still grinning when he turned, the sound of his mother's laughs and squeals as they tickled her following his ears as left.

"Father," Xillik said in greeting, closing the door behind him. Xavier, though now old, was still as foreboding as he always was. His shoulders were broad, his arms were still muscled, and his hair was gray and long, matching his beard. He was hunched over as his eyes scanning the map in his hand that he had snatched from his desk. No doubt taking it in with a critical eye to better tell him everything Xillik was doing wrong.

"You lost land," his father's deep voice rumbled, not sparing him a glance. And as always, the undertone of his disapproval made Xillik's spine stiffen.

"It was plagued with fire, drying it out. Our crops would no longer grow on it."

Xavier didn't say anything, just picked up the next document and scanned it.

"You allowed some of our people to move."

Xillik gritted his teeth, trying to hold back his ire.

"I'm surprised to see you," he said, evading. "I wasn't expecting you and mother to visit."

Xavier's lips quirked, wryly. "You would have preferred for us to send message of our arrival." Xavier looked up from the map to meet his gaze. "Why?" he asked, his tone mocking. "Need time to hide your mistakes?"

Xillik held his stare, expressionless. But his insides were heated, both in indignation and the useless childish hurt of disappointment. He was a grown man, had been chief of the Izayges for four of his twenty-four winters. He shouldn't crave his father's approval, but he did.

He always did. Even if knew he would never get it.

"We can't all be as perfect of a chief as you, father."

"Don't be so childish," Xavier scoffed, throwing the maps down on the table. "This isn't about perfection. It's about you losing valuable land and people of the Izayges. It's about you losing crops that the entire tribe depends on."

"There was a fire," Xillik gritted out. "I am not the Gods. I cannot control their will of nature. This is not my fault."

"It is your fault!" Xavier roared, slamming a palm down making everything on the table ratttle. "You are a Chief. You need to expect every situation, ever disaster. You need to have back up plans for your back up plans. You need to be ready. For everything! And you rebuild. Always. No matter if the destruction was caused by Gods, or mortals."

Xavier exhaled roughly, turning away from him. He surveyed the desk once more before coming from around it. Xillik stayed still, matching his glare with his father's when he stopped in front of him. He was taller than Xavier, but in his presence, in his disappointment, he felt two-feet tall.

"You need to be better, Xillik," Xavier said quietly. "I didn't let you be chief to fail and undo everything I have worked my entire life to accomplish."

"I never asked to be Chief," he snapped.

"But you *are*," Xavier growled. "And I expect you to be better."

Xillik looked down, and with one last angry sigh, his father left, bumping his shoulder with his own as he did.

"I can't be you, father."

He heard Xavier pause, holding the door open.

"No, you can't. You will never be the chief I was."

He waited for the door to close before he lashed out with his foot. It collided with the leg of the table, breaking it and causing it to topple forward, spilling everything at his feet.

"How much do you want to bet Xi and Da got into it?" Hunter murmured from his spot at the table. Rhoxon and Ryder turned, watching the stiff way their older brother and father stood next to each other as their mother talked. They were no stranger to their brother and father's relationship. Every time Leawyn and Xavier came to visit, Xillik's mood changed. Sometimes lasting for days after they leave.

"Of course, they did," Ryder snorted. "They always do."

"Cut him some slack, ya?" Tyberious scowled, grabbing another chicken leg. "It's not like uncle has ever given him a reason to be glad of their visits. You know he only comes to tell him every way he isn't a good chief."

"Kind of like you?" Trixus grinned.

Tyberious socked his brother in the arm while the table snickered. Tyberious was only three years younger than Xillik, and like their brother, he took over being chief of the Siraces when he was twenty.

"Hey, where's Lévaunia?" Titus, the youngest of Tyronian and Namoriee's children, asked, causing pause to the punching fight his brothers started with each other.

"We haven't seen her," Ryder said.

"We've been looking all day," Rhoxon added.

"Oh, really?" Hunter drawled, side-eying them. "Is that why I saw you two pounding Ifle earlier today?"

"Shut up!" the twins shouted at him.

"Why must you two literally do *every*thing together?" Titus grimaced.

"Aww don't worry baby brother," Tyberious smirked, clamping

him on the shoulder with both hands. "You'll bed a girl eventually."

They whole roared with laughter that only grew in volume when Titus got up, throwing a dirty look at them as he stormed out.

"YOU KNOW EVERYONE IS LOOKING for you?"

Lévaunia glanced over her shoulder briefly before looking back, not replying. She ran her fingers through Killie, her bird's, feathers as Viktorious came and lowered himself to sit next to her.

He tipped his chin to Killie. "How's he doing?"

Lévaunia smiled. "Better," she replied. "Should be able to fly soon."

One day when Viktorious and her were riding in the woods, they came across a fallen nest. Killie was the only one to have survived, though just barely. She defied nature by taking him to try and heal him. They hadn't even known what kind of bird it was. It was a long shot, but the baby bird ended up surviving and though his wing was broken, she refused to believe that Killie wouldn't be able to fly again.

Viktorious nodded, turning his gaze to the sun that was setting. They stayed in companionable silence for a long while, neither of them feeling the need to fill it. Lévaunia loved all her cousins, but if she had to choose, Viktorious would have to be her favorite. He shared the same quiet intensity with her uncle, Tristan. His skin was a lighter mix of his mother's, and he had dark—almost black—straight hair that came down past his shoulders before he had shaved it off.

They were similar in a lot of ways. They were the only two to have dark hair in their immediate family, though she had blue eyes and he had gray. He was the only one who never pressured her to talk, and though protective like all her brothers and cousins—she was the only girl after all—he was never overbearing about it.

He accepted her, because he knew what it was like to be different.

"My father wants me to marry," she said quietly. She felt Viktorious's stare, but she couldn't bring herself to meet his gaze.

"Wants you to marry…or ordered you?"

Lévaunia looked up at him. She didn't have to tell him the answer.

"Your mother allowed it?"

She shook her head, giving him a sad smile. "My mother may be able to sway my father on many things, but…"

"Not this."

"No," Lévaunia whispered. "Not this. His will is law, and I must abide by it."

Viktorious shook his head. His expression rarely changed, always a mask—just like her uncle's—but she knew him. She could read him better than anyone. Because while his face was expressionless, his eyes were not.

They always gave him away.

And right now, he was feeling sorry for her.

"I knew it would come to this. I'm the only girl in this entire family. I shouldn't be surprised. If anything, I should be happy. At least I grew up with my betrothal."

"Who is it?"

"Cixrus"

An angry scowl twisted Viktorious's lips. "That whore? Why would he do that?"

She shrugged. "There's no way he would betroth me to someone in the Izayges, not with all my brothers around."

"Your father is a fool. Cixrus won't give a damn about you. He's between more legs than the twins."

"Don't be unkind, Vik," she reprimanded softly. He shook his head, looking away from her angrily, though she knew his anger wasn't aimed at her. She gave him a moment to compose himself.

"When?" he asked finally after a long pause.

"On my eighteenth winter. Just like my mother."

"I'm sorry."

"Me, too," she replied sadly.

He wasn't apologizing for what he said.

"Lay! Hey, Lay. Lay, stop!"

Lévaunia sighed in irritation but slowed her steps enough for the person who called her name to catch up to her.

She turned to him. "My name is Lévaunia, not Lay."

Cixrus grinned, coming to a stop too close to be considered appropriate.

"I'm going to be your husband—I get to call you anything I desire."

Her lips thinned, but it was the only indication she showed outwardly of her disgust. She ducked away from his hand when he tried to touch her cheek.

"You aren't my husband." She told him simply, taking a firm step back. It did nothing to deter him, he only took another toward her. She refused to back away from him again, so she stayed still when he pressed his lips close to her ear.

"*Yet,*" he told her. "You have two more winters of freedom, baby chief. Then you're gonna be mine." He pulled away with a grin, looking down at her. His gaze grew heated, serious. It made her nervous.

"You have pretty lips. They as soft as they look?"

Her eyes widened, his intention clear when he lowered his face to hers. Luckily, he was stopped before they could get any closer.

"Get away from her," Viktorious snarled, coming out of nowhere. He shoved Cixrus hard enough that he stumbled back a few steps before he found his balance.

"Nice to see you again, Viktorious," Cixrus smirked. "How's

Vida doing?"

"Vik, don't!" She said sharply, holding him back by his arm when he took a threatening step forward. There was a time that Viktorious and Cixrus were friends, but that all changed when Viktorious caught Cixrus in bed with Vida two years ago.

She was Viktorious's first love, and Cixrus was her first lov*er*.

"Get out of here before I break every bone in your face," Viktorious told him in quiet fury.

"I'd like to see you try."

"Vik!" Lévaunia cried, sliding forward on her feet, still trying to hold him back when he lunged at Cixrus.

"It's not worth it!" she cried hopelessly when Viktorious shrugged out of her grasp and grabbed Cixrus by his collar. Viktorious's elbow pulled back, fist at the ready.

"There a problem here?"

Everyone froze.

"Lévaunia, come here," Xillik ordered his sister, pulling her to him by the arm he placed around her shoulders when she did so right away.

"I'm sorry, Xi." His sister's whisper was soft, only a few octaves lower than her normal tone. For having four older brothers, you'd think she'd be more boisterous to match the craziness, but she wasn't. No, his dear sister was soft-spoken. Gentle. *Innocent.*

It was her innocence that he wanted to protect. They were all protective over her—she was the baby after all—but he wasn't ashamed to admit he was more extreme when it came to his duty as eldest brother.

He pulled her closer to him, leveling a glare over her head at the bastard who almost succeeded in kissing her, if it wasn't for his cousin.

"Well?" he barked, his angry gaze flickering between Viktorious and Cixrus, who were locked into their own stare down.

"No," Cixrus snapped, shrugging out of Viktorious grip forcefully. He took a step back, keeping his angry glare on Viktorious. "There's no problem here."

He looked to his cousin. "Vik?"

A silent war waged between Viktorious and Cixrus for tense moments until Xillik was convinced that he would have to break up a fight after all.

"No," Viktorious gritted out finally, breaking his stare to look at him. "There's no problem here, Chief."

He felt his sister relax with a sigh, but he didn't do the same. "Good. I would hate for our guest to have to go to a healer."

His cousin smirked at his insult. But Cixrus knew better than to try and correct him. Instead he gave him a tight smile, before his eyes switched to his sister, who was half-way shielded by his bulk.

"Enjoy it while it lasts, Lay."

Xillik's humor died at that cryptic threat, but he held up a hand to stop Viktorious when he took a threatening step toward Cixrus. His eyes followed his every move, and once he was out of sight, his sister moved so that she was next to Viktorious.

"What was that about?" he snapped, looking between them two. His gaze narrowed when his sister and cousin shared a look between them then looked back at him. They spoke simultaneously.

"Nothing."

"Don't lie to me Nia," he said, calling her by the name only he used.

His sister shot him a fake smile, wrapping her arms around his waist in a hug.

"I've missed you brother."

Xillik hummed, unconvinced. He knew that she was just trying to distract him. His arm wrapped her up tight, hugging her back anyways.

"You're a brat," he told her affectionately, admitting defeat.

She giggled, the cute sound always able to make him smile.

"Everyone's been looking for you."

"So, I've been told," she said in wry amusement.

"We've missed you. You don't visit as much as you use to."

Her expression turned sad, and it pained him. His father might have been strict with him, but he was downright overbearing when it came to Lévaunia. Once it became apparent that she was going to be more beautiful than his mother, with her raven hair, flawless complexion, and sparkling cobalt eyes, their father changed. All the sudden, Lévaunia stopped coming to visit them. His father was protective, as they all were, but...there were days when he felt like his father treated his sister more like a prisoner than a daughter.

But for whatever reason, his sister didn't see it that way. So, he kept his mouth shut, because you'd have to be blind to not notice the amount of love she had for their father, and he for her.

Not that it was saying much; Lévaunia was a lot like their mother in the way that it was impossible *not* to love her. He didn't think his baby sister had a mean bone in her tiny five-foot-two body.

"I'll go find them. Besides, I'm worried if I don't soon, the twins will find some unique way to punish me," Lévaunia laughed. She gave him one last squeeze, going up on her tiptoes to give his cheek a kiss—he still had to bend his body at the waist for her to reach—before pulling away from him to do as she said.

He waited until she was out of earshot to turn to Viktorious.

"So, you going to tell me what that was abou—"

Xillik's mouth slammed shut with irritation. Viktorious was gone—an annoying habit Viktorious had learned from his father Tristan—and he knew that his minx of a sister was to blame.

Lévaunia had distracted him long enough so that Vik could slink away, knowing he would interrogate their cousin as soon as she left.

"Damn it."

"No," Xavier gritted. "Absolutely not."

Leawyn sighed, setting her brush down and turning in her seat to look at him.

"Why not?"

"Because, she's sixteen Leawyn. She's not old enough."

She raised a brow. "That's what you're leading with? Really?"

Her husband for many decades scowled at her. "The answer is no."

Leawyn rolled her eyes, turning her back to him and continued to brush her hair.

"Lévaunia hasn't spent nearly enough time with her brothers as she should have. You've kept her locked away like a sea monster guarding his treasure. Well, she's not some possession—she's your daughter. She deserves to be with her family."

"We are her family," he pointed out grumpily.

Leawyn slammed the brush down and shot to her feet, whirling around to face him. She was inwardly smug at her husband's wince when she did so.

"They are her brothers. You just sold her off to be married on her eighteenth winter, to a different tribe, where I know more than *anyone* means that she will not be able to come and go as she pleases to visit her *family*. She deserves some freedom, Xavier!"

"She is free!" he yelled.

"No, she is not!" she shouted back. Xavier's gaze narrowed, leveling her with a look that that had long since lost its effectiveness with her.

"You need to let her go, Xavier. You need to understand."

"She isn't unhappy," he said, frustrated. "She agreed."

"Xavier," Leawyn sighed sadly. She moved to him, cupping his aged cheek with her hand, playing with the fine gray hairs there.

"She loves you. She might have agreed, but don't for one instant believe that you didn't just crush her whole world the moment you traded her freedom from your will, to his."

Xavier closed his eyes, pained. He pressed his forehead to hers.

"I just want her to be as protected as she possibly could be. This is the only way I know how."

"I know you believe that," she whispered sadly. She closed her eyes, too, pressing a soft kiss to his lips.

Xavier gripped her cheek, keeping her from pulling away by deepening the kiss. He wrapped an arm around her, pulling her up against him as he walked them backwards. Their lips only left each other's long enough to pull their clothes away from their bodies. He lowered her down, his body quickly following.

"Xavier," Leawyn breathed in pleasure when he slid into her waiting warmth slowly. He peppered kisses on her cheek, her neck, while his hips started a slow rhythm. Pumping inside of her with slow, unhurried strokes. No matter how many times he's taken her over the years, it always felt like the first time.

His need was never sated for her, and hers for him. It was never enough for them, no matter how many times they had made love with each other over the years of their marriage.

"Say it," he panted against her damp skin, nipping the juncture of her neck and shoulder. Her nails raked down his back until they gripped his toned ass, pulling him in closer. *Needing* him closer. He picked up his pace, holding her tightly in his arms.

"Say it, Leawyn."

"I love you," she gasped, arching her neck in ecstasy. "I will always love, Xavier."

"I'll find you, even in death," he whispered into her ear, choked with emotion.

Leawyn sobbed, clutching him to her as she climaxed, bringing him with her.

The next morning, before they left to return home, they told their sons and daughter that Lévaunia would live with them until her eighteenth winter.

Xavier didn't feel the need to tell them about her betrothal, and she didn't feel the need to remind him.

Because she had a hunch he did that purposely.

EPILOGUE

THE SUN WAS SETTING, BRINGING A chill in the breeze that Leawyn didn't feel, even as it caressed her skin and hair. Everything within her was numb. Her sons, Xillik, Ryder, Rhoxon, and Hunter surrounded her, standing close. Xillik on her right, Hunter beside him, with the twins behind her. Her youngest was on her left, clutching her hand tightly. She could feel the tremors wracking her daughter's small frame as she tried to quell her crying, but she couldn't bring herself to comfort her.

She couldn't bring herself to do anything but watch through dead eyes as Tyronian and Tristan stepped forward. Their expressions were etched in grief as, together, they gave the boat that was on shore a shove, trudging through the waves and sending it away.

Her eyes never left it, even as Xillik turned to her.

"You should do it," he whispered roughly.

She looked up at him slowly. His eyes, so much like his father's, glistened with the promise of tears he refused to shed, but his face was otherwise expressionless. Her boy was strong. Not because he wanted to be, but because he knew he needed to be. She smiled sadly, resting her withered hand upon his cheek, while the other grasped what he offered. His eyes closed, accepting her silent comfort, and his moment of what he thought was weakness. When they opened again, the emotion in them from before was gone.

Warrior eyes.

With a nod, he stepped back, and resumed his place among his siblings. She stepped forward, notching an arrow as she went and dipped it in the fire, making sure it soaked the oil. Her hands, though old and weaker than in her youth, didn't shake when she pulled the bowstring back.

The fire made a flickering sound when the arrow released, and it took mere moments for it to land. It created a small flame within the boat.

There was a moment of silence, then the sky lit up with the valley of flame-tipped arrows that flew overhead, hundreds of them following the path that hers did before.

Wordlessly, she watched as the boat carrying her husband's body engulfed in flames; burning away his flesh, and with it…her heart.

Everyone had left.

His father might not have been the most compassionate man, but he was respected greatly. It seemed that half the villages of the other tribes showed up to his funeral. His family had stood with him. All his uncles, and cousins, and siblings, Torrick and Alissowyn and their children, Kade and his wife.

Everyone was there.

They had stayed long after the sun set, but slowly, the crowd began to disperse until only his kin had stayed with him, but they, too, began to leave. His uncle Tristan being the last. He clapped his shoulder, red-rimmed eyes meeting his. No words were spoken between them, because they didn't need to. He knew.

Take care of her, his uncle's eyes had said. *She needs you now.*

Xillik stared at his mother's back, who was standing in the same position she was in after she shot the first arrow. Usually, it was the eldest son who would shoot the first ceremonial arrow for the fallen warrior chief. But, his family was never one to follow traditions, and it would be foolish of him to start now.

Everyone knew that the rightful honor belonged to his mother.

His mother, who's grief was more potent than his own. He studied her, as if he was seeing her for the first time. His mother's beauty was a thing of legend, something that never diminished. But now, he was starting to notice things that had been there from the beginning, but that he was too ignorant to see.

She had always been small, tiny even. But now as he looked upon her, she seemed frail. Breakable. Her hair was long and floated in the wind, the gusts blowing the strands that were once bright blonde, but now a dull white. Her spine, which had always stood tall, and proud, was now bent; folded over in age and despair.

He hated it…but he expected it.

When word was sent that his father was fading, he had rushed to his side. But by the time he got there, his mother was clutching his body and sobbing.

He was too late.

He had been sick for months, Namoriee had told him.

His parents never said a word.

It all happened in a blur after that, and now here he stood. On a beach staring after a woman who stared after a boat that had long since burned away.

He sighed quietly, giving himself a moment to compose himself and gather strength for what he would have to do, before he moved.

"Mother," he said softly, grabbing her hand. "It's time to go back home."

It was like she didn't even hear him.

"Mother," he pleaded. Squeezing her hand in his. "Let me take you home now."

She ignored him, and just when he thought he would have to forcibly carry her away, she showed the first sign of life by speaking.

"He *was* my home, Xillik," she said, the words dripped with sorrow so profound it made his eyes sting.

She didn't say anything else, just turned and allowed him to escort her back to her room.

It was silent between them, even after he helped relieve her of her shoes, and tucked her into bed, pulling the bed-furs high to her chin. He treated her like a child, and it broke his heart because she was anything but. He kissed her brow, but the hand on his cheek stopped him from standing after he pulled away. He met his mother's gaze.

"He was proud of you."

He tried not to let her words affect him, to let her see the bitterness he could taste in his mouth.

He tried to smile, but couldn't. "I know in his own way he was, mother. You don't need to do this."

She didn't reply, just scanned his face like she was trying to etch it into her memory. "I know he put pressure on you. He expected more from you, so he pushed you harder than any of his other sons. But he *was* proud of you, Xillik, because you are the leader he never could have been."

"And what kind of leader is that?"

She smiled sadly. "*Kind.*"

Emotion clogged his throat, and he had to swallow it down so that his voice didn't crack when he said, "get some sleep." He kissed her cheek again before standing. "I'll check on you in the morning." He blew out the candle by her bed and turned for the door.

"Xillik," she called, prompting him to look back at her. "I'm proud of you, too. You were my first great accomplishment. You know that, right?"

He smiled. "I know, mother. Your love was never something I questioned."

His unspoken truth made her expression turn sad. He never

doubted his mother's love, but he did doubt his father's. It was a secret he would keep to his grave, sans this moment. It made him feel weak, like a little boy pathetically vying for his father's approval that he knew he would never give.

"Watch out for them," his mother said, bringing back his attention. "Especially Lévaunia."

He frowned, a few urgent steps propelling him forward. "Mother—" he started, worried.

Something about her tone made it seem like a goodbye.

"She's suffering, Xi. He was the sun to her."

He nodded in understanding. His father and little sister shared a bond that none of his brother's shared. He had only see him father show tenderness a few times in his life, and it was always with his mother or sister.

"I'll always watch out for them. Just like I'll always watch out for you," he promised. His concern grew when his mother's eyes glistened with fresh tears.

"Please don't cry," he said softly, coming to her bedside again. She grabbed his hand from off her cheek and held it, staring him in the eyes.

"I love you, Xi. You're a good son to worry, but I'll be fine soon."

Her last sentence confused him, but instead of responding, he simply accepted the kiss she gave his cheek. She dropped his hands with a squeeze when he stood, and with one last wish of goodnight, he closed the door and left.

When he came to collect her the next morning, she was gone. No one said it out loud, but they didn't have to because the last thing she said to him made sense now.

His parents shared a love that no one had understood. It was brutal, passionate, and true. They were two beings who shared a soul, however broken they might have been.

Leawyn couldn't live with half of her soul gone.

His father was her heart, and it refused to beat without him.

... for reading *HOW THEY FELL*!

I am new author, and any reviews are very much appreciated. If you have a few moments to spare, I'd greatly appreciated it if you left a review on the retailer's site where you purchased the book, and send the review link to contact@authornicolerene.com and I'll personally thank you with a written response!

OTHER BOOKS BY
NICOLE RENÉ

FALLING WARRIORS
They don't love—they own.

Want to know more about Xavier and Leawyn and their beginning?
Check out their book and first installment of the *Falling Warriors* series in
HOW THE WARRIOR FELL.

A complete full length novel available exclusively on Amazon and Kindle
Unlimited.

Buy it here.

http://bit.ly/howthewarriorfell

Please turn the page to enjoy a little taste of *How the Warrior Fell*.

HOW THE
WARRIOR
Falling Warriors Book One FELL

Nicole René

SYNOPSIS:

SHE was the Chief's daughter in a small tribe...

To bring an end to an ancient feud between her tribe and another, Leawyn's hand in marriage to Chief Xavier was the only way to ensure peace.

HE was the fiercest warrior of them all...

Plucked from everything she's ever known, and bound to a man she hates, Leawyn must learn to be strong. Each passing day renews Leawyn's longing to escape, but when a new threat from a mysterious foe puts the tribes in jeopardy, everything changes...including her feelings for Xavier.

Bound between duty and honor, Leawyn must make the decision that could change everything. Can she stay and accept her new life, and her husband? Or is Xavier's heart too cold for her to melt?

Lines will be broken.

Blood will be shed.

With love being their biggest battle of all, only time will tell, if it will be enough...to make her warrior fall

Author's Note: This book is a Dark Historical Romance and as such may include themes that are uncomfortable to the reader like arranged marriage, graphic violence, non-consensual sex, and an over-the-top alpha warrior who is extremely possessive and demanding. Being historical, it is written in accordance to the views and laws of the time period.

EXCERPT

LEAWYN STARED DOWN AT HERSELF in the basin of water, her sea-blue eyes taking in her hair that fell around her heart-shaped face in thick, long waves. She touched her cheek and trailed her fingertips down to her pale pink lips. Leawyn sighed and swiped the water in the basin roughly to erase her reflection.

Her head snapped up at the sound of footfalls coming towards her room.

Oh Gods, they're coming, she thought. Moments later, the flap separating her room from the rest of the hut swung aside and in stepped her father and betrothed. She gasped softly when the man's cold brown eyes met hers.

Xavier kept his merciless eyes focused on her as he stood to his full six-foot-six height. His coal-colored hair brushed the tops of his broad shoulders, spread wide against his defined chest. His arms were bunched with muscles as they rested against his sides. The rumors she heard revolving around this man were all true, Leawyn realized, because looking at him now, all she could think of was danger.

Leawyn could still feel the heavy weight of Xavier's gaze as she looked over to her father, who spoke suddenly, breaking the tense silence.

"Daughter, this is your betrothed, Xavier," Boers said nervously as he glanced to Xavier before looking at her again. "Chief of the Izayges."

Leawyn looked to Xavier again, the heat of his gaze making her uncomfortable. She lowered her head, dipping her body slightly at the waist in greeting.

Xavier continued to study her, raking his eyes up and down her body slowly. She felt even smaller in front of him. As discreetly as possible, Leawyn peeked up at him and studied him much like he did her.

His broad chest was bare, and he wore dark breeches that looked to be made of some type of tough animal skin, similar to leather. She could only spot three noticeable weapons on his person, but she doubted it was all he had on him. He had a sword that was long and wickedly curved strapped to his back, and another long, thick, straight blade hung down from the side of his waist. On the other side of his hip, Leawyn could see the hilt of a dagger peaking out of the waistband of his breeches. She glanced at his arms. They were massive. She looked down, heart rate spiking.

He was terrifying.

"Leave us," Xavier demanded gruffly. His deep voice caused the demand to come out more like a growl. Leawyn felt her eyes widen, glancing at her father in fear.

Don't leave me, Leawyn thought.

Her father shifted uncomfortably, but nodded his head. "Of course." He bowed to Xavier. Giving his daughter one last apologetic look, he turned and lifted open the flap of the tent, leaving Xavier and Leawyn alone.

Leawyn lowered her eyes back to the ground, her chest tight with dread. She heard Xavier move closer to her, and she took a halting breath against the nervousness that seemed to choke her and keep her body paralyzed.

"Tell me your name, girl," Xavier demanded, staring down at her small form. She was tiny compared to him. He easily towered over her.

Leawyn felt herself bristle slightly at his tone. He didn't ask, he commanded.

"Leawyn," she answered softly, proud her voice didn't come out as shaky as she thought it would.

Xavier's expressionless mask twisted into an angry scowl.

"Look at me," Xavier growled, his voice low. When Leawyn's eyes failed to meet his fast enough, he reached down and gripped her chin and jerked her face up to look at him.

"Your gaze will always meet my own," he told her sternly, staring down into her wide eyes. "You will only have eyes for me, do you understand?"

Leawyn's feelings of fear quickly turned into annoyance. "Shall I call you master while I'm at it?" she asked sardonically, glaring at him defiantly. She wasn't prepared for the sharp jerk he gave her chin as he forced her to tilt her face up higher.

"I do not appreciate the attitude, Leawyn. You will do well to remember who exactly you are talking to, and you will respect me," Xavier growled down at her, yanking her chin up yet again, and causing a whimper of pain to escape from her.

"Now, do you understand?" he asked again. When she went to give him a nod, he tightened his grip on her before she could follow through with the motion. "The words, Leawyn. I want the words."

"Yes!" Leawyn gasped out against his tight hold, staring up at him with wide, frightened eyes. "Yes, I understand!"

Leawyn rubbed her aching jaw as he let go of her abruptly. She took a few steps away from him hastily, trying to blink back the tears of pain and fear that clouded her eyes.

"How old are you?" Xavier asked, watching her.

"E-eighteen summers," Leawyn stuttered, looking up at him nervously. She knew he was much older than she, and the knowledge that she was expected to marry him made her stomach clench with sickness. But, Leawyn knew some girls younger than herself were married to much older men. She told herself she should be somewhat grateful.

"We will be married in three days' time."

Leawyn's body tensed in shock, the icy cold feeling of dread washed over her. "What?" She gaped at him. "We can't!"

She couldn't live with this man! This possessive, domineering man who didn't care if he hurt her.

She shook her head. She wouldn't marry Xavier. Not after meeting him.

"I will not marry you," Leawyn said suddenly, her brows creasing as she stared up at him in determination.

Xavier stiffened, every muscle in his body tensing as his eyes cut to hers. Leawyn swallowed against the urge to run as she edged away from him, catching the dangerous glint that entered his eyes.

The glint was that of a predator who caught sight of its prey right before attacking.

She had a feeling the prey was her.

"What did you say?" Xavier asked, his voice was silky and dripped with promised danger.

Leawyn gulped, but then lifted her chin defiantly while staring at him with more bravery than she felt.

"I will not marry you," she repeated, backing away from him as he took slow, measured steps towards her.

Xavier shook his head slowly, his icy eyes never leaving hers. "I'll ask you one more time, Leawyn. What did you just say?"

"I refuse to marry—"

Xavier's eyes flashed furiously, his hand shooting out and wrapping around the back of her neck in a vice-like grip. Using his other hand, he gripped her jaw brutally.

"You will become my wife, Leawyn," he said in warning. He leaned in, rubbing his bearded cheek against her smooth one. "And if I find out you have let another man between your legs come our wedding night…"

She could only emit a soft gasp of pain as Xavier's grip around her neck squeezed tighter.

"I'll kill you," he whispered softly into her ear.

Leawyn sucked in a sharp breath, and he laughed humorlessly as he drew back and looked into her frightened eyes.

How had her life come to this?

Available here
http://bit.ly/howthewarriorfell

Want to know more about Tyronian and Namoriee's love story? Check out their book and the second installment of the *Falling Warriors* series in **HOW THE WARRIOR CLAIMED**.

A complete full length novel available on Amazon and all other major retailers.

BUY IT HERE.
http://bit.ly/HTWCbookbuylink

Please turn the page to enjoy an excerpt of *How THE WARRIOR CLAIMED*.

Author's Note: This book is a Dark Historical Romance and as such may include themes that are uncomfortable to the reader like arranged marriage, graphic violence, non-consensual sex, and an over-the-top alpha warrior who is extremely possessive and demanding. Being historical, it is written in accordance to the views and laws of the time period.

SYNOPSIS:

He was the chief's cousin.

Namoriee knew the only way to protect herself against the blond-haired gentle giant was to stay away. The way her heart pounded and her insides fluttered when he was near could only lead to disaster.

Two years ago he made a promise to her that she never thought he intended to keep.

She was wrong.

She was the handmaiden.

Tyronian wanted Namoriee even when he knew he couldn't have her. The need to possess her was so deep, it took every ounce of mental and physical strength he had to keep the promise he made to her that stormy night.

He promised he would wait until she was older.

He promised her two years.

But now… time's up.

Namoriee wants nothing to do with him but he has no plans on stopping until she's in his bed, and he's in her heart.

She *will* be his. Forever.

Whether she likes it or not.

EXCERPT

Namoriee hurried away from her Lady Chief's hut, keeping her eyes on her feet as she passed the people in her village, dodging bodies as she went. She felt a slight moment of guilt for leaving Leawyn when she was still recovering, but she couldn't stay in that room.

Not with him in it.

Only when the sound of her village dimmed, did she let out a sigh of relief.

She turned her gaze up to the sky and closed her eyes in contentment as the sun's rays bathed her face, causing her body to relax completely.

"You shouldn't be out here alone."

Namoriee jumped, whipping around to stare at the blonde in front of her who was frowning at her disapprovingly.

"The woods aren't safe these days," Tyronian told her, and as if to prove his point, his blue eyes scanned the tree's suspiciously before they came back to rest on hers.

She stared up at him silently, not knowing how to respond. She moved back a step when Tyronian moved one forward.

Noticing this, he took another step towards her. When she once again stepped back, he stopped, grinning.

"You're not afraid of me, are you Namoriee?" he asked, voice light with his amusement.

She stiffened. "No, I am n-not afraid of y-y-you." She lied, her eyes taking turns between flashing up to his face and the ground.

"Really?" he drawled, arching a brow.

Namoriee's hackles rose at his tone, causing her to lift her chin up insolently. Her eyes flashed with emotion she rarely demonstrated.

"Yes, really!"

He grinned, amused at her show of defiance and false bravado.

"If that is true," he drawled, casually taking another step closer to her with an indulgent grin quirking his lips when she tensed but forced herself to hold her ground.

"Prove it." He purred, stopping so that their bodies were just a breath away.

He must have felt her chest rising and falling quickly against him with her rapidly beating heart; see her lips part slightly at their closeness. Could he smell the scent of her sweat from her hard work around the village?

They were so close that she could feel his warm breath against her cheek, the edges of his blonde beard scratching against the top of her head. His heavily muscled frame encompassed her tiny, frail one, shadowing her like a waterfall would with a rock. His presence was nerve-wracking, and it was all she could do to not let him see how much he affected her.

Her limbs were trembling, caused by an emotion she didn't quite understand. Whatever it was, she didn't like it. She needed to get rid of him.

Now.

Namoriee squared her shoulders and tilted her head so that she could better look him in the eye.

Gods, he was massive! Just how tall was he?

"I believe I am, and have already," she replied boldly, proud that she didn't stutter with her nervousness.

He chuckled, and leaned his elbow against the tree he managed to back her up against, just beside her head and trapping her in.

"Yes, you didn't retreat. Good job, Namoriee."

She took a sharp intake of breath as he dipped his head so that their face were level with each other, pinning her with his gaze.

"How long will that last?" he challenged in a whisper. Her eyes widened.

"I-I don't know." Namoriee said, stumbling over her words, his proximity making her nervous and causing the hairs on the back of her neck to rise with awareness.

His lips were so close to hers—another centimeter and they would be touching.

He studied her quietly, and her eyes had a war on where to look— his eyes, or his lips. He stared at her not as a man measuring the prospect of a horse, but of a man of studying a sword being made. He looked at every detail, taking in every flaw and perfection.

She felt exposed, and self-conscious.

Her hair was lighter than the other women in the tribe, more of a chocolate color than coal. She was frail, her skin tanned from all the days she worked outside in the sun. He towered over her; her forehead level with his chin.

Finally, he met her eyes, taking in her expression.

"Do I make you nervous, Namoriee?" he asked quietly.

"Y-yes." Namoriee replied, just as softly. She closed her eyes when he leaned closer and trailed a finger lightly down her cheek.

His lips brushed against hers when he asked his next question, voice a low murmur.

"Are you afraid of me, Namoriee?"

She inhaled deeply through her nose, opening her eyes that clashed with his vivid blue ones. Her lips trembled when she whispered her answer.

"Yes."

Tyronian said nothing for a moment, and both continued to stare at each other in tense silence. It was as if the air sparkled with electricity, so potent, you could feel it.

He straightened slowly, and dropped his arm from the tree. Turning his body sideways, he gave her the space she needed to slip by and escape him.

Tyronian stared after Namoriee as her long brown hair flew out behind her like a whirlwind as she ran.

Away from him.

She was young, too young even. The fact that he was eleven years her senior should have been enough to keep him away, but it wasn't.

He couldn't.

"I'm sorry," he whispered to the empty space she was at a moment before.

Because he knew…he wasn't going to let her run away from him for long.

She was doomed long before this encounter because he had already made up his mind.

She was going to be his. Forever.

Whether she liked it, or not.

Available here

http://bit.ly/HTWCbookbuylink

Acknowledgments

As always, to my family—thank you for always being so supportive of my me and my dream to become an author. You never give up on me and always push me to be a better writer, and a better human being. I love you.

To Heather Ambrose—Girl, I'm so happy to of met you at that LA signing! You truly have become a friend, and your constant support and enthusiasm of my books is everything. Here's to many more books and years together!

To my betas and review team— Thank you for riding this crazy rollercoaster that is the world of publishing and being an author. Your excitement makes me excited, your love for the characters and story makes me fall in love with them all over again, and your critiques, notes, and general kick in the butt makes me the best author I can be. Thank you, you ladies rock!

To Tiffany with T.E Black designs—Oh. My. God. THIS COVER!! Thank you so much for your brilliant design skills and giving me one of my favorite covers! Can't wait to keep working with you!

To my warrior tribe—Ladies, you make my day fun. Thank you for your support. I might be bias, but I think I have the best readers ever.

ABOUT NICOLE RENÉ

NICOLE RENÉ IS A SAN Diego native living with her grumpy kitty, Sebastian and her crazy cute Boxer, Walter.

When she's not busy creating sexy alpha males, you can most likely find her with her nose stuck in a book reading OTHER sexy alpha males, kicking back with her friends and family, at the movies, or further fueling her "The Little Mermaid" and "The Lord of the Rings" obsession.

She is a certified klutz, often tripping over invisible objects, dropping things like they were hot, and playing ping-pong with the walls. She has lots of tattoos, loves to eat sushi—but hates eating cooked fish, hates going to the beach (even though she's surrounded by them), and is still waiting for her Hogwarts letter to come in the mail.

***

Want to be in the loop and know what's next? Sign up for my newsletter and always be informed about upcoming books, new releases, sales, exclusive sneak peaks, giveaways, and much more!

https://landing.mailerlite.com/webforms/landing/u3x9w9

I like to procrastinate using social media. You can add me by click on the links below.

www.authornicolerene.com

AMAZON: http://bit.ly/nicolerenesofficialamazonpage
FACEBOOK: http://bit.ly/authornicolerene
INSTAGRAM: http://bit.ly/atauthornicolerene
TWITTER: http://bit.ly/atitsnicolerene

Or join my warrior tribe on Facebook here
http://bit.ly/warriortribegroup

www.ingramcontent.com/pod-product-compliance
Lightning Source LLC
Chambersburg PA
CBHW052007170626
46808CB00007B/2808